94

Bracknell's Law

A JOAN KAHN BOOK

Bracknell's
Law

Wallace Hildick

HARPER & ROW, PUBLISHERS

NEW YORK, EVANSTON, SAN FRANCISCO, LONDON

A HARPER NOVEL OF SUSPENSE

Bracknell's Law

Her Journal:
Entry Number 1

If Ron can keep a special diary all hidden away, you'd think it was a woman, why shouldn't I, so here goes. Maybe I'll get some kind of thrill out of it, some kick, you never know your luck. No but seriously, when I found the book I got the shock of my life, or I did when I got into it and read some of the things he'd put, because at first I just felt how sweet it was really, keeping one of his old schoolbooks all these years and all these miles, somehow I felt touched, it *was* touching, but then—well—well here I am at it myself.

Mind you I'm not saying I can write it down as elegantly as he can, I mean he did have the education for it and then there's the practice, all the reports he has to make, hour after hour, night after night, up in the attic bedroom he uses as a den for writing in, except of course it wasn't always *business* reports, we know that now, don't we, yes. But never mind, just imagine you're writing a letter home, Pat, the ones they say sound just like me talking, that is what I have told myself, and already I feel better for it, now I've started, and it really truly does seem the best thing at this stage. I mean it's not something you can talk about to anybody, even your best friends, and even if I was back in England even then I don't think I could bring myself to *talk*—really talk about it—not even to Mum—well especially to her—but—well.

Anyway. Let's face it. I am worried. Really. Not as shocked as I was at first. But very worried. Not that I think for one moment he *means* all that, good heavens no, my God, but even if he doesn't—I mean *though* he doesn't—it's a bit, well, it's a bit peculiar to say the least. Unhealthy. And he *has* been working hard these past two years, ever since we came to America, not that he didn't work hard before, but it's been doubly hard since then like coming up from behind, like being handicapped, like Ron says you have to be twice as good, like you were black or something, and well, there it is, it's not been easy. Not for either of us. I try to tell him that, but.

Anyway.

Where was I?

Begin at the beginning, Pat, that's always best. Miss Sinclair always used to say that at school, so first the book I found this morning no first the way I came to find it because believe me, whatever I am or aren't I'm no snooper, even Ron has never been able to say that about me though he's said a heck of a lot of other things—or *looked* them which is just as good when you've been married thirteen years—these past two years.

No. It was quite by accident. As sure as God's my judge if it hadn't been for Mr. Jones I would never have found out and even when I did find it, well it was only an old school notebook, there seemed to be no harm in glancing through it and trying to imagine what your husband must have looked like, been like, when he was thirteen or fourteen.

Mr. Jones is a carpenter.

Not just any old odd-job man, Mr. Fixit, no sir, though you wouldn't think it, I mean you wouldn't think there was so much difference until you had him in your kitchen after waiting a week to fix that window the Grady boy next door broke with a baseball and then you happened to mention there was this tap I mean faucet that had been dripping and was now getting worse by the hour.

"Do you know anything about taps, Mr. Jones?"

"Taps, ma'am?"

This was the first time I'd spoken while he'd been fixing the new pane of glass, because you never know, get them talking and they take hours longer than necessary, and although he doesn't *look* the gabby type—he's long and thin and yellowish and gray, where I find it's the darker ones who seem to have so much to talk about—I wasn't taking chances.

"Sorry," I said, thinking I could kick myself, talk about giving him a handle conversationwise, next thing it'll be "You British?" as if he didn't know, and "I was there during the War" and so on—"I mean

2

faucets. The cold one there. It's not that I haven't turned it off, it's the best I can do. And with the cold weather coming on."

He clamped one of his big bony hands over it and turned but it still went on dribbling and I thought good, now he's hooked, now maybe I'll get it seen to.

"Yeah," he said. "Needs fixing. Nothing to it. Just a washer."

"Oh," I said, making it sound vaguer than I felt because of course I knew it was a washer, it was getting the damn thing put *on* was all, "Oh," I said, "is it very difficult? I think I have a new washer here somewhere, now let me see, yes, here."

"Nergh!" he said. "Anyone can fix it, ma'am, it don't need a plumber. Just tell your husband, when he gets home, he'll know. He's—"

"Yes, but—"

But Mr. Jones was talking now and he meant to go on talking, I could tell the way his eyes were twinkling, nice eyes, clear blue, beautifully clear for a man his age—what, 50? 55?—under the shreddy eyebrows.

"He—heh! heh!"—laughing in his throat, deep and soft—"guess he's been putting it off, huh?" *Now* I thought he was leering, *now* I thought oh God I'm sorry I spoke. "Coming home tired, all that hard riding on the train after all that hard riding behind a desk, doesn't want to know about no faucets needing fixing. Don't blame him, myself. Mrs. Jones is always getting on to me, same thing. But when he sees how bad it is he'll fix it all right. When—"

"But that's just *it*, Mr. Jones. He"—I knew I was taking a risk here, but still, I mean there he *was*, on the spot, and if it really was as urgent as that I'd only have to call on some other man, some neighbor, and believe me the problems would still be the same, this neighborhood—"he won't be back until the weekend, Mr. Jones."

"Oh?" He was leaning against the sink now, absent-mindedly still tugging at the tap I mean faucet, all set for conversation, you could see it in his face. "Traveling man, is he?"

"Sort of, yes."

"Heh!"

"Is that something funny?" I said, deciding to crisp it up a little, nothing like a touch of discipline to keep things from getting out of hand.

"Huh? No. No, ma'am. . . . Just an old joke I was thinking of.

This guy on the plane: I travel in ladies' lingerie. Other guy: Yeah, well, I don't blame you, this hot weather we been having."

"He deals in packing materials," I said, not laughing, making out I didn't quite hear him. "Bonding strips," I said, hoping this talk of mechanical things would bring him back to the matter in hand. "Strapping. Steel strapping. Actually he's more of an adviser, technical adviser. Just now he's up in Buffalo and he won't be back until Friday, so—you think this will be O.K. till then?"

Mr. Jones rubbed his jaw. The mention of Ron's job being something technical like that, something in his own line in a way, but very much more advanced, this seemed to steady him, make him more respectful.

"Nuh-huh," he said, looking doubtful at the tap. "You got a pipe wrench in the house?"

"Excuse me?"

"Pipe wrench. Or a monkey wrench would do. Then I could fix it myself."

Well thank goodness for *that*, I thought.

But I still didn't know what it was he was requiring.

"What kind of wrench would that be?"

"Like—like a letter F," he said, and I didn't like to look to see if he was leering again, "which can be adjusted to grip hold of a pipe," I felt myself starting to blush, "or in this case a nut, a packing nut."

"I know what you mean," I said, trying to sound nice and calm and cool but wondering what I'd been letting myself in for, "my husband has one, I'm sure of it. In his—er—toolbox."

"Yeah, well, do you want to fetch it in here, ma'am?"

"Don't *you* have any"—I nearly said tool but changed it to anything—"anything that will do the job?"

"Me, I'm a carpenter, ma'am. I don't carry plumbing equipment around with me. Your husband take his tools with him then?"

It was a straight question, no smut, so I gave him a straight answer:

"No, it's not that. It's just that he's very proud of his tools, you'd think they were the Crown Jewels—"

"Aren't we all, ma'am?" he said, looking more respectful than ever, and nodding. "Aren't we all? But he won't mind me using his wrench. A plane maybe, or a file. But not a wrench. Not on a two-minute job like this. Not a trained craftsman. Not in an emergency, which

4

this is gonna be if it ain't fixed before the weekend. So if you'll just bring it to me—"

"But that's just it, Mr. Jones. I would. But he keeps the box locked, padlocked. Ever since I used a chisel to open a packing case one time."

He winced, then was grinning again.

"Padlock, huh? Well now, equipment for padlocks we do have, ma'am." And he stooped to his own bag of tools and came up with the biggest bunch of keys I ever saw. It turned out that half the jobs he was called out for were to do with opening locks someone had lost the keys for, and rather than break those locks, weakening doors and damaging furniture and things, he always tried his keys out first. "Nearly twenty years it's took, building this collection," he said, down in the basement, in front of Ron's big steel box, trying one after another of the smaller keys. "And you'd be surprised how many—yeh!—heh!—there! Y'see? Fifth attempt. Nothing to it."

The lock had sprung open. He took out the key and stood back.

"It's all yours, ma'am," he said.

Well I could see it was a matter of principle with him to go so far and no farther, and somehow I got the impression that this went for all departments of life too, so I felt easier about turning my back on him and took the lock off and lifted the lid and pulled down the front edge of the box to show the three narrow drawers, but we didn't need to open any of them because the wrench was among those exposed on the top in their little fitted beds. And now he was *very* respectful because I must say Ron does keep his tools as if they were the Crown Jewels, talk about gleam and glitter, and when Mr. Jones pointed out the one he wanted, still standing well back, he did it with his little finger and in a hushed sort of voice.

"That should do it, ma'am."

Well I must say, although I knew that Ron was fussy about his tools—obviously!—the effect it had on this other man, and a trained craftsman at that, made me see them in a new light, even made me feel something well up inside me, something warm such as I'd never felt for years, for Ron I mean, not just sexy though there was that in it, I don't mind admitting, and the result of it all was that I stayed down there awhile after Mr. Jones had gone up to fix the faucet, and I just touched the tools here and there, just lightly, stroking them (now! now! not in that way!)—no, just feeling respectful myself and kind of gently loving, and then I tried the drawers, the top two

5

first, with all their smaller items, even shinier, like silver some of them, and then the bottom, and that's where I found the book with all these old school experiment reports in the first part and then in the later pages, in Ron's own recent handwriting, all these other reports, also of experiments, but not about the effect of heat on various metals and the angles of light on prisms and mirrors and all that, oh no, but about—well—why wrap it up, the subject of these later experiments—all about different ways of killing.

Killing people, I mean. With dates and times and places.

As if he—Ron himself, my Ron—had actually carried them out.

And as if that wasn't upsetting enough, how about this?

At the end of each set of notes there was a newspaper clipping stuck in there, describing how the bodies had been found all matching up with those dates and times and places, places I knew he'd been in or near, during his travels, it hasn't taken long to check.

Her Journal:
Entry Number 2

I'll say this. Writing things down makes you think more clearly. Slows you down a bit, I suppose, gives you more time, just that fraction, pins you down (now! now!).

No. Seriously. Since writing all that first lot, this afternoon, I've been doing more thinking than I think I've ever done in my life before except maybe at school, or no, that was just sort of mechanical, not for real, simply exams and tests and that, so, well, let's say except for the time just after we first came here, when everything was so strange and when the novelty had worn off and things needed thinking about, believe me.

But hold it, Pat. Whoa, gal. Let me keep things in order, one thing after another, the way it happened, as Miss Sinclair used to say when we wrote about what we had done during the school holidays, or The Happiest Day of My Life (when I wrote about being a bridesmaid at my cousin Evie's wedding, not so happy for some) or A Day in the Life of a Sheep Dog—things like that. "You're very good with Content," Miss Sinclair used to say, "but your Expression, Pat, needs—"

All right. All right.

It's with thinking of Ron, his schooldays, on account of that book, this book (I've got it here now, right in front of me), must be catching.

Well. When Mr. Jones left this morning (you should have seen the respectful way he wiped that wrench on one of his shirt sleeves, undoing the button to get a better stretch of cloth to wrap around before he handed it back)—well, after he'd gone and I'd put the wrench back, I didn't snap the lock back into place, of course not, plenty of time till Friday evening. No. I left the lock off altogether and took the book out and really settled down to read it, not skipping or skimming, and all through lunch I read it, taking care not to let any crumbs get into it because believe me it was, is, spotless, even when he was a kid he must have taken care of his things, I mean nothing, no blot, no stain, only the edges slightly yellow, with time (something even he can't keep away).

So then, after I read it through once, and even though I read it fast it took me nearly two hours, what with not skipping anything and sometimes having to stop to look up words, well then I decided to do a bit of writing myself. And the reason I decided that was— no, I'm going too fast and I tell a lie. I didn't read it, *then* decide. I didn't even decide just like that, no. It just seemed to creep up on me while I read Ron's words, so—back to the book. Let me describe that first.

It was, *is*, a fairly thick book, quarto size, I mean British quarto size, ten by eight, and I didn't have to take Ron's shiny steel ruler out of the box to check that information, no sir, not after all the ten-by-eight sheets I pushed through the machine back in the office back in England, seven years of it, my God, in the Concentration Camp we called it, never mind Typing Pool, but that's by the way. So. Ron's book. Stiff-backed, dark olive green, neat label neatly centered:

R. W. BRACKNELL, 4A, GENERAL SCIENCE

—and not a fancy border doodled in, not likely, not our Ron, but aw, I thought, because being nice and neat and clean in a kid is something else again, you can appreciate it in a child, it's different when you're not married to it. So aw, I thought, I wish I could have met him then.

And inside, neat, so neat. Everything. The writing, the underlining, the little diagrams, the tables, blue-black the writing, red the underlining, black ink the diagrams, black ink the borders of the tables, it must have taken him hours. (I'm talking about the front part of the book now, you understand, the reports on the science experiments and that.) As for the Content, well science we didn't do that kind of science at my school and what bit we did I hated, but honest the way Ron had written it down it even began to look attractive to me and I might even have kept the box open to read about the school experiments even if there'd been nothing about these later experiments if that's the word.

Just for example, take one of the last entries in the first part, called *Resistance* and dated nearly twenty-five years ago which made him just about fourteen at the time (I must remember to go downtown and get him something for his birthday). *Aim*: it says, *To determine the relationship between the current in a wire and the potential difference between its ends.* Just like that, nice and straight out, you don't have to know what the words mean to realize little Ron knew exactly what he was after. Then *Apparatus* it says, and under it, indented just so, you'd think he'd done it on a machine, the left-hand margin straight as that:

Accumulator
Key
Rheostat
Ammeter
1 meter Eureka wire (S.W.G. 28)
Terminal board
Voltmeter

I mean excuse me, but it may seem nothing to do with it to anyone else but to me, that list—so pat-pat-pat (hey, now I come to write *that*, maybe that's what he saw in *me*, the name itself, Pat)—but no, seriously, to me that list *is* Ron. Ron then and Ron now. With its dead-straight margin and its fancy words and its *exactness*. (I mean I bet he didn't *have* to write all that about the wire.)

So then to the next heading, step by step: *Procedure*.

We connected (*we*—I'd love to have seen them at it, seen his partner, bet *he* didn't have much say either) *the accumulator in series with the Eureka wire* (AB) (there's the neatest little sketch with all this of course, every line as straight as straight except where there's a deliberate wiggle, which believe me I bet he measured out and did it with a pencil to be sure before inking it in, and a couple of circles which he did, not with a compass there's no prick—hey! hey!— but probably by penciling around a dime, or no, it would have been a sixpence of course, silly me!) *through a key, rheostat and ammeter, and connected the voltmeter* (V) *across AB. We switched on the current—*

And so on. And again, for "we" read "I"—you can bet on it.

"Hey, Ron, let *me* do this bit!"

You can just hear his poor little partner. And him not saying a thing, not even letting on he's heard, just getting on with it, step by step. Oh yes, I know about Ron and his Procedure. Even in bed—but now, now, keep the party clean, Pat.

So on to the *Results*, which at least there *were* some with *that* partnership, all set out neat, three rows in a table under the headings *Current, Potential Difference,* and *P.D./Current* (which I nearly wrote down as *R.B.* over *Partner*—well, not really, but honestly it's uncanny). And then another heading: *Conclusion.* Ron all over once again, one of his favorite words, always drawing conclusions. *It was found that the fraction R.B./Current was constant*—there, I've done it.

Anyway.

Anyway, come on, Pat, we can't stall any longer, anyway then comes the second half of the book. No headings, or not many, no fancy diagrams, no different inks, just the one blue, but the same old Ron, even the handwriting the same only smaller, firmer, flowing more, more determined, driving, God that drive, even the Americans notice it and some of them don't like it, believe you me, and I sometimes feel like telling him, loosen up, Ron, or simply just *pretend to* for God's sake, it'll pay dividends, but no. *Him,* listen to *me?* Ha!

So here we are, with these reports, death death death, kill kill kill, and damn the resistance *he* ever seems to meet, which proves I guess it's really only in the mind, like sex when you think of that, but what got us onto *that* again? But anyway, you will be seeing for yourself.

Because after thinking about it, after reading and thinking, I decided to do this writing myself, because, well, let's face it, *Ron is sick.* Must be. I mean I don't think for one minute he's really done any of these things, I mean he probably reads the news reports first and then works backward, just as that Ohm's Law thing existed first before he experimented with the wire and ammeters and things, yes, that's it. But.

But what a subject! What a Content!

And the Expression sometimes—well, you'll see.

Sick.

So if he's sick what about me, where does that leave me? High and dry is where if it gets worse and he has a real breakdown, but not only that, it's my duty isn't it? In sickness and in health. And the best thing I can do is to get it all down, so I can go over it and over it, even after he comes back, *especially* after he comes back, because come Friday evening of course the book goes back in the box and the lock snaps back on the lid. This way I don't have to worry about that and, if it comes to it, I'll have an exact record to take to someone who might be able to straighten it all out.

So bear up, Pat. You'll probably end up with writer's cramp but it's better this way. You certainly couldn't take the book to that place downtown near the library and get it xeroxed because what if the clerk should look over your shoulder, or if there's some sort of copy retained in the works, and they believed it was true? Oh no! Not in this country where the police are ready to believe anything and where they'd probably use it against him even if they didn't believe him, just to clear up their records, oh no! I may be called Pat but I'm not having my husband made a Patsy, no sir.

And anyway, copying it all down, nice and steady and faithfully (a fair copy is an exact copy, as that old bitch Miss Compson typing-pool supervisor was always saying), doing that will be like reading it all over again very carefully, it will help me think, and what the heck it will help pass the time as well, so after supper here goes with Killing Number One complete with General Introduction by his nibs the Executioner (no, though, mustn't laugh).

His Journal:
Entry Number 1

Bracknell's Law. That is what it might very well be called.

I first got the idea just over two months ago, when I fasted for a week. There is no need to go into details here, of course. They are largely irrelevant. Suffice it to say that it was the culmination of a period of maximum frustration, especially at work. I felt angry, humiliated, even to some extent intimidated, and I reacted blindly, oddly. I stopped eating and, apart from water, drinking.

Initially this was understandable enough. I felt too choked to eat. Literally fed up, I suppose. But after that first half-day, even when my appetite began to return, I kept it up. It was protest, pure protest, real protest, nothing to do with the sort of crap the papers are currently giving a capital P to.

No. This was gut protest, with a vengeance, an organic revolt against the revolting. And no sulking was involved, either. Mark that, because it is important. To sulk presupposes an audience, an onlooker, a witness—someone to be made to feel guilty. And I mentioned the fact to no one.

At work they thought I was lunching alone somewhere. (It was one of the weeks I was back in the office.) At home my wife believed, variously, that it was because I had been lunching heavily, or because I was simply off color. She had no idea I was not eating anything away from home anyway—and she is not the fussy type. About food, at least.

So I kept it up for a week, which was days—three days, four, at least four—after I was craving for food. But I kept it up. I stuck it out. And I kept quiet about it. And why? Because—it became apparent to me—because it was something none of those bastards could ever do. Not while putting in a full week's work. Not while remaining silent about it. Furthermore, it lost me weight that I could well do with losing, so I didn't even have the chagrined feeling of cutting off my nose to spite my face. In other words, I had put their nastiness and stupidity to good use. I had *made* those bastards do me a good turn.

The effect was remarkable. The effect was noted.

It was not just the loss of weight. It was something much more important than that. It was something internal, the inner triumph, and it showed. It showed in my behavior—I very soon saw *that*—and they reacted accordingly. For not only had my self-respect been restored by this very private course, it had been given a very powerful boost.

It wasn't long afterward that I entered the second stage—a couple of weeks, three at the most. And it came, surprisingly enough, in the shoddiest of guises: through the pages of a cheap paperback, a novel about the Mafia. It was a passage (one of those pseudo-documentary snippets they seem to love to sprinkle their pages with nowadays) about the disciplinary effect produced on one's associates and acquaintances and so forth by the knowledge that one had killed before and would be prepared to do so again. Usually (it was pointed out) this fact—the fact of a killing already accomplished—renders further killing unnecessary.

Well, that is a commonplace enough notion. I must have read or heard it scores of times before in this and similar connections. But, coming as it did this time so close on the heels of my experiment in fasting, I was able to see it in a new light. There was, in effect, a catalytic reaction between the two ideas. In short, I got to thinking that possibly it was not just the actual direct knowledge possessed by acquaintances that had this effect on them. Perhaps there was also something in the *presence* of the killer—some sort of vibrations, some psychical emanation—set up or created by his *own* knowledge of the fact.

Is that so outlandish?

That is what I asked myself. And I came to the firm conclusion, based on my own recent experience, that it was not. A man who has killed and is prepared to kill again must *look* different. Strangers, not knowing anything of his career, must sense it. The fact that he himself knows must effect some chemical (yes, I'd go so far as to say that, speaking now with further hindsight)—some *chemical* reaction in his personality.

Now. Here was food for speculation.

I proceeded to think of all the times one *feels* like killing. Or at least, not to press the point, *approaches the threshold of feeling like killing.* Because of course we are conditioned, and have been so for generations, to suppress such ideas immediately they begin to stir. Is it not likely then that such repression has its chemical reaction too—particularly in people without the power to punish or control or exert influence in other, so-called civilized ways by virtue of status, say, or relationship?

I think so. I think it more than likely. And I further think that in this case it is a *bad* chemical reaction, quite the opposite of the enhancement of self-respect discussed above. A manifestation that results in skulking, ratlike, muttering behavior and attitudes. And in fear, too, let us not forget that. (Because even when confronted with those we might feel like killing for healthy reasons—bullies of one kind or another, rapists, say, muggers—we are inhibited, and the law encourages this inhibition.)

However, that is another question. The negative aspect interested me much less than the positive. I pursued the positive line a little further. Thus:

Supposing one had killed, and the aura was there, would the people one had felt like killing still behave toward one in the way that makes one feel like killing them?

There would be no question of direct intimidation, it must be understood. Just the aura, the vibrations, whatever. Would that suffice?

Well, it seemed feasible. The more I thought about it, the more I believed it to be the case, and the more interesting and then more exciting became the idea of an experiment. But what of the objections?

Let us take them in order.

Morally, first. No case. How many killings are done indirectly but nonetheless effectively (dead is dead) by the general public, the innocent-in-the-street? I mean through idleness, for instance, through the failure to check a certain part of a certain aero engine, say, or even to check a suspect tire before going onto the thruway?

14

Or simple human vindictiveness through the usual human channels. ("Fire him! I don't like the way he spoke to me just now." Or: "No, I don't want you back.") And all this quite apart from direct legal methods, in war or in anti-criminal activities. There is nothing intrinsically morally wrong with killing, unless one is a pacifist, and I am not. And besides: if one is selective, who knows how many other lives one might save by taking the right one? It is a thought we shall return to later.

Practical objections next. Put quite simply, the overriding question (given one's willingness to experiment) is this: *How to get away with it?*

Well, thanks to Bracknell's Law (the inner reflection of the physical act, the *public-oriented* inner reflection of the *private* physical act) there is no great problem. The field is opened up, folks! For one would not have to kill those who had actually offended one; only those similar to those who had offended one. (And God knows they are legion!) Thus there would be no direct link, no motivational chain, for even the most assiduous detective to trace. Indeed, there would not even be a special pattern, as in the case of sex criminals, for instance (women of a certain type, a certain age, a certain coloring, etc.), or as in the case of homicidal maniacs, who tend to attack similar types in set ways and so build up an operational picture, a sequence that can eventually (but even then only with luck) be determined and used as a lead.

Further: there need never be a killing in high-risk circumstances, or in one's own neighborhood, or in any usual haunt. No dragnet-hazard factor, to coin a phrase. Since no particular person is ever being stalked, one can afford to await the ideal opportunity.

Further: weapons can be varied. The gun, the knife, the doctoring of some apparatus, the doctoring of some food or drink, the accidental stumble culminating in the fall (of the other!) over a cliff—anything and everything effective can be used without much fear of their being incriminating later, each instrument being bought or stolen or otherwise procured for the specific job and then abandoned. Naturally, such details as fingerprints one would have to be careful about, but even they need cause no great anxiety to someone who knows his prints are not on any record.

They say the police shudder at the very idea of the indiscriminate killer, precisely because of this very difficulty in tracing the motiveless, or the only vaguely motivated, or the secretly motivated, perpetrator. Well, with someone putting an unknown law into effect, a completely new concept in modern killing, they might well have something to shudder about. Later, maybe, when the posthumous reports are published and the carbon copies begin to appear, the police may develop special techniques:

"Calling Victor One, calling Victor One. Proceed immediately to the corner of 86th and 3rd. Bracknell-type killing reported. . . ."

Meanwhile, shudder on, Joe Friday, Lieutenant Erskine, Chief Ironside, Charlie Barlow, Steve Carella, et al.! Because for a traveling saesman such as the original Bracknell, with a moderately wide freedom of movement, the experimental conditions couldn't be more favorably set.

One further objection, before proceeding to the first of what I trust will be many fruitful experiments, and again it concerns method. No matter how indiscriminate one may be, or seem to be, in the choice of a victim, and no matter how favorable the circumstances may seem, a physical appearance has to be made when conducting the experiment. It need not be an actual confrontation (killing by remote control is something one may well consider worth investigating later, by the way), but a *significant presence* must be effected somewhere along the line, sometimes. What then of the blunderer onto the scene, the stumbler into the act, the chance observer? Must one crown that experiment with a further killing?

Possibly.

Probably.

One must always be prepared for such accidents. Certainly one must begin by revising one's views about sparing innocents. Do the armies and air forces of the world? Do the quick-reacting policemen when returning the fire of rioters or rooting out skyjackers or other ransom artists? *Always?*

In extremis, then, we should have to see.

But that is by the way. Because one is so seemingly indiscriminate, the innocent get to have a bonus. One victim of a certain type is just as good as any other, after all, so that with the approach of a possible witness the experiment may be cheerfully enough abandoned. There will always be the comforting thought that it can be set up again elsewhere, and reasonably soon.

Which brings me to yet another bonus vis-à-vis the chance of interruptions—and this time it is for the experimenter himself.

Because there is no madness in this, no sadistic hankering after watching the death throes of a victim or hearing his pleas, no dirt of that kind, one can afford the luxury of killing by the delayed-action methods touched on earlier, with death taking place when one is hours and miles away. So: let who wants happen by at the critical time. And anyway, even when death is immediate, the choice of place will almost invariably be such that the body will remain undiscovered if not concealed for at least a commensurate stretch of time.

Theories, theories . . . They are all very well, but one has to make a practical start somewhere. That is the greatest hurdle. Simply to find out if one is *capable* of making such an experiment. Of taking the first small step that is, truly, such a giant stride. Well, I am a great believer in easing oneself into such situations. The simple exercise first. A safe and satisfactory little lollipop of an exercise, as it were (in its practical aspects, that is). Something to break through the barrier with one-hundred-percent safety, yet with the boost and boon of certain initial success.

That is why I decided on poison.

A coward's method?

Not when making one's first experiment in the field, surely. It takes courage to kill for the first time, be well assured. Just to kill. No matter how safe one might be from all possible detection and punishment by outsiders, one is aware—if one is reasonably intelligent and civilized—that the *inner* dangers, the instinctive reactions, are likely to be great. Will one be able to bear the thought afterward? How will one's nerves, one's whole system, react to the knowledge that one has succeeded? It is an irrevocable step, you must understand, the first small step in *this* field. There is no way back. The very thought of it puts one in mind of the old mumbo-jumbo about making pacts with the Devil, and suddenly it doesn't seem such nonsense any more. I know I had such thoughts. But I felt equal to them. And so I proceeded. Because that's what it is all about. The name of the game. Bracknell's Law. All right?

Poison, then: the means.

And the victim?

"Oh, just this once," I told myself, "practically anyone will do, so long as it isn't the sort of innocent that will feed the reaction you wish to avoid.

17

"Never, in fact, choose an innocent for a direct subject, whatever your views on dealing with the innocent witness, who may never cross your path."

(That last point might well be a prime corollary of Bracknell's Law, incidentally.)

"So for this first essay," I told myself, "why not take a leaf out of old Dostoevsky's book? Some worthless flotsam, a tramp, hobo . . ."

And then of course I had it.

Poison?

A *wino*, what else?

That was the week I was going to be in Cleveland and I thought I knew the very spot.

Her Journal:
Entry Number 3

Well, that took longer than I thought, I must say, and I still haven't got to the Killing, never mind though. No, but I was up until midnight copying it out and then I couldn't sleep for it, thinking about the time he was talking (writing) about and trying to puzzle out just when. But not to worry, I think I have it worked out, and it is still only Wednesday and I've canceled my hair appointment.

So.

So well, as I say, it was very late last night when I finished copying that lot out and I must say for all the sleep I got I might as well have gone on copying. But it is important, Pat my girl, I keep telling myself, more haste less speed, and like I said (wrote!) yesterday writing things down does help you to think more clearly, makes you concentrate if you see what I mean and not only that. One other thing.

Copying things out helps just as much.

Because it makes you take it slower and more carefully and I'll tell you this. Copying all that out of his seems to have given me a new view of Ronald, a new angle, not only in what he thinks about or *did* think about but in the way he looks at things and the way we are different.

Like his writing compared with mine. I mean the Expression, the way he puts things, the words he uses, the punctuation, all that. I could never write so just-so, so beautiful you've got to hand it to him, in a million years.

But more than that. I mean like it makes it very clear when you are writing exactly the same thing (and it isn't just the fact of having to do it on the sly, I mean he must have had to do it much quicker and more furtive, I mean with me being in the house which I'm pretty sure is where he did it when he was supposed to be writing his business reports—*do not disturb, on no account disturb me, no calls, nothing*—and

Oh hell!

See what I mean?

I go off the rails, I lose track. And if you start something in brackets don't forget to close them, Pat, no, Miss Sinclair, there.)

No though. Not only a question of handwriting, which doesn't really enter into it here anyway, but the more important things. Take the words he uses. Some of them I had to look up, and that takes time, not that he doesn't use fancy words when he's just talking to me or to anyone in the company, but those times I don't have the chance to look them up.

"No, stop, Ron. Hold it right there. Don't say another word till I have looked that one up."

Hah! You can imagine the black looks *then!*

So no, I've just got into the habit of pretending to understand and letting them go, water off a duck's back, and that way, I can see now, I haven't really been knowing my husband all these years. Oh dear! And no wonder we . . . Oh well. But now to work.

Not copying any more just yet. It came to me last night in bed to try to remember, cast my mind back, to the times when the Killings were supposed to have happened, well *did* happen I guess, judging from the clippings. But I mean when Ron was supposed to have done them or *believed* he had done them, I don't know, but you know what I mean. But then then *then*. To think about *then*. And his behavior then. Around the time.

And see if there are any links.

So here goes.

As near as I can make it, this part he was referring to would all be fourteen to twelve months ago. Because the more I think about it the more I think I know when he did that fasting. (Fasting!) I don't remember it *as* fasting of course, because as he says, he didn't make a song and dance out of it (honestly, the things men do on the sly!) but I remember one particular week, well several days, when he was off his food, which isn't like him at all for all he's so thin, Mr.

Hollowlegs my father used to call him. "Get married quick, Pat, or he'll eat us out of house and home."

September it would be. Just after we'd come back from vacation, yes, that would be it, because I remember thinking it might have been something he ate up in that restaurant in Montreal, dirty French, except there'd been a gap of about a week and I rather fancied food poisoning struck quicker.

Yes.

Writing it down *does* help fix things.

Yes and then I remember thinking it must have been the heat in New York, worse even than the summer, that had something to do with it, and maybe we should have gone south not north for the vacation, just when he seemed to be acclimatized and all.

Yes.

And then after that I had to admit it must have been the Old Problem, what had become the Old Problem anyway, and that was things were going just as badly at the office as before the vacation.

Badly here as well, I should add. Because be honest Pat this was the end of our first year in the States and things had been going from bad to worse for months. Then

But begin at the beginning. How about that year? Because it wasn't all gloom and misery, now was it? Be fair. From good to bad to worse would be more like it. Or even Beautiful to good to bad to worse.

Well, all right.

The big mistake, let's face it, was making our home here, Palmers Rotten Point (the middle bit's what *I* call it). If we'd stayed in New York, like we did in the first two weeks, God that was wonderful, like a fairy palace, a fairy city (now! now!—I don't mean that kind of fairy, though I must say—well, anyway) I suppose it was because we'd read and seen so much about it and it came up to all our expectations and then some.

Anyway.

Anyway be fair. No one was to blame. Palmers R. Point itself also seemed wonderful at first, especially that time of the year, blazing fall, nothing like it, I'll never forget that drive up the Merritt Parkway. (Sly old Raybourn, going that route, instead of the Turnpike or the railroad which after all poor Ron would have to be the one to endure, day in day out.)

But anyway we loved it, and we loved the weekend at the Ray-

21

bourns' (my, how Sylvia must have worked on her smile to keep it up for two whole days, the two-faced little bitch) and *that* seemed a dream too, not as glittering as New York but let's say *glowing* shall we, yes glowing. All those smiling faces (five parties in two days!) and the leaves, yes glowing. And then even when we moved in, the glow continued, oh yes, with lots of people helping, smiling, welcoming, the honeymoon wasn't over.

I tell you everything is wonderful in a new country at first. Even shopping for furniture. Even sitting in the yard. Even driving downtown for a dental appointment. Even coming out of the dentist's with a numbed mouth and thinking how much better it all was the way they did things over here, first name first sentence: "Well just sit in the chair, Pat, and we'll see how things are." (Cheeky devil, I thought, I'm not having gas with him, but then I didn't know that they all do it over here, even doctors, first name first name all the time and it doesn't mean a thing. Or correction. As Ronald said, after *he'd* grown tired of it all, "They do it just to get a better grip on one," and believe me he was right. When I think of that slimy Charlie Raybourn and that snake-in-the-grass wife of his! Steady, Pat.)

So all right. Wonderful, wonderful. For about six months, wonderful. The Britishers, that was us. The British are coming, the British are coming! The way they used to yell it out when we arrived at the parties. All winter it was parties. The Raybourns, give them their due, saw we met everyone there was to meet, and invitations came from all quarters. Talk about thorough. Looking back now I marvel at it, all the different sections we got to meet. I mean the Yacht Club lot as well as the Beach Club crowd. Even the P.T.A. people, even though we'd no children.

Yes, the Raybourns worked hard. Had to, I suppose. They'd got us into this. They were our sponsors in a way. He was Ron's colleague at work, in a way his boss, higher up anyway, though not directly over him. Fat Charlie Raybourn with the little green eyes, doing a little empire-building according to Ron, or intending to, planning operations on the train, sowing seeds, stirring trouble, or intending to.

Well.

Some fell on stony ground all right.

Anyway.

The Raybourns worked hard. Yes. But also it was this British thing, something new for the Palmers Pointers just as the place was something new for us. And, just as we were studying Palmers Point, weighing it up, weighing them up, so they were studying us through all those parties and get-togethers, all through winter, weighing us up, and finding us wanting just the way we were finding them wanting.

Be fair though.

Who was it led the way? Really and truly? Who was it first began to show how they felt?

Still, shouldn't they have allowed for that? Shouldn't they have understood how *exhausting* it is to uproot yourself at that time of life, leave friends, relations, home, job, country and start over, in your mid-thirties, three thousand miles away? And how, being exhausted, you're not ready to give parties yourself or always be ready with the smile and that stupid kidding stuff, twisting words round, which we left off with our school blazers? And how even if you weren't go goddamned tired, or sapped, it would be a year or two before you had the money, what with the outlay of starting a new home, and in *this* place, for God's sake!

Sure they should have allowed for it. It would do some of them good, uprooting like that. Why, most of these bitches are here because they're shit-scared of living in New York and that's a fact even though it is swearing.

I'm sorry. But they can still get me mad when I think of it.

And Ron felt exactly the same way. Exactly. I don't usually know exactly what that one is thinking (you can say that again, Pat!) but this time I did because we came right out in the open with it one afternoon and we said so, confessed it to each other, and I shall never forget it because it was such a relief because he'd been coming home all tight-lipped and I was beginning to wonder if it wasn't all my fault. So I remember it particularly well, one Sunday when we were due to go to a party at the Zetlingers', spring it was, a lovely afternoon, and "Sod it!" he said.

"What?" I said, partly because he'd said it so softly, standing looking out the window, and partly because it is unusual for him to swear nowadays.

"I said sod it," he said, still with his back to me.

Oh dear, what have I done now? I thought. But I wasn't going to show it. I said very firmly:

"Sod what then? What is it *now*?"

"That party," he said.

23

"Which party?" I said. (After all, there were three coming up, wider-spaced than at first, but definite invites, the Raybourns were still working hard.)

"Tonight," he said. Then he turned and I could see it wasn't me he was mad with. "Can't we get out of it?"

"Get out of it? Now? It's only another three hours away," I said. "How can we do that?" Then, improving the shining hour, I said: "I know what you mean though. Don't think I'm not getting as sick of them as you."

"You are?" he said. "Honest, are you?"

The way his eyes shone. The way he grabbed my arms and gripped me. God! My heart looped the loop. We'd been getting so tired lately, and getting to bed so late, we hadn't had time to. But that's our business, I suppose.

"Yes," I said. "I am. And I'm beginning to get uneasy. I get the feeling that they're saying things about us. About not having parties ourselves."

Then he said "Sod 'em!" again and started saying some of the things about being exhausted and the money and that which I've mentioned already.

Oh, how glad I was to hear that!

"So that settles it," he said at the end. "We're not going."

"What!" I said. "But—but we must."

"Must?" he said, and his eyes got glittery. "No one says must to me."

I thought he was kidding.

"No, Your Majesty," I said, but he gave me such a look I shut up real quick.

And do you know, we didn't go to that damned party. And do you know what excuse he gave? He picked up the phone and he called May Zetlinger and he hinted, no he more than hinted, that I was four months gone and had come over all queer and he'd called in some specialist in New York who'd asked him to drive me down to his office right away, right that very afternoon.

I mean imagine!

Me, at thirty-five, no children before.

And the Zetlingers with six, and Harry Zetlinger always making cracks about how the British Obviously Were *Not* Coming. He meant it the sex way of course, "But this one time," said Ron, putting down the phone, "he will have to take it"—what's the word he used—oh yes—I can see him saying it now—"literally."

Then he got out the car and we went for a drive in the country, way inland, and found a place called the Ward Pound Reservation where it reminded us of parts of England and then we had a marvelous meal at a country inn and it was lovely.

And over the meal, over the wine, Ron said:

"And this settles it. We will move to New York. Palmers Point is only for schmucks and family men."

But of course it wasn't all that easy. We'd committed ourselves heavily. It would take time. We might even have to wait another year and even then bank on him getting promotion.

"But we'll do it," he said, holding my hands and squeezing till I nearly cried out. "Oh yes, we'll do it."

And that's where things started going from bad to worse.

Not right away.

Right away we had this baby thing to untangle. People started getting more interested. The Zetlingers sent flowers the very next day. I felt a heel, I really did, and the more people inquired and kidded and made kind offers the worse I felt a heel and that didn't help, because quite obviously Ronald didn't feel at all a heel and was enjoying it and then I started nagging him, asking him to kill the rumor, and then he didn't enjoy it so much, and even when he said he would put it around that I'd miscarried it wasn't any better because I refused and said it was terribly unlucky to use things like that for excuses and then he got on to one of his contemptuous kicks, thinking (I could read his thoughts, he didn't have to say it) how he should have married a college girl and not some superstitious little slut from the typing pool and we had one of those horrible Silent Rows he sometimes goes in for, not Sulks, no, but Rows Without Words, just looks and shrugs, and oh it was horrible, but I never expected him to put an end to it the way he did.

God!

Then he thinks he has *brains*.

I ask you.

Telling Raybourn straight out one morning on the train. No I wasn't having a baby. No there never had been chance of one. No it was just as excuse that afternoon.

So then it went from worse to worse and worse, all through the summer, with people getting very bitchy and Raybourn himself quite snotty, even at work, especially at work, and coming right out with it one day and telling Ron that we'd been letting him and Sylvia down, and so on, up until the vacation, and things so bad then that we were too uptight to even begin to unwind, everything seeming knotted up, and then coming back and then—yes, it was then all right—this fasting which I've only just found out about.

Followed by a change in him. Yes. Oh very clear now. Not just thinner. More—more compact, more vivid. Lips tighter, eyes always more glittery, actions quicker, more definite, more *purposeful*.

Not happy. Not that. But not despairing any more, not even irritable. But very, very determined, very purposeful.

And Cleveland, yes. I remember him going up that way that time. It was a week. Rochester, Buffalo, Cleveland.

But of course I never dreamed what thoughts were churning around and around in the poor lamb's head.

Just listen (I mean read) this next bit, if you please!

His Journal:
Entry Number 2

1. *The Venue:* Cleveland railroad station, main concourse.
2. *The Agent:* Barbituric acid.
3. *The Vehicle:* 1/3 bottle, cheap Scotch.

NOTES ON ABOVE

(a) The venue. The main hall or concourse of a railroad station immediately recommended itself because, while being the natural haunt of various bums and winos, etc., it is also much frequented by people of all kinds. In other words, a "square" would never obtrude there as he might in a Skid Row area. Furthermore, the general bustle and the natural preoccupation of most users of such places offer excellent automatic safeguards against one's being noticed.

But why not one of the big New York terminals: Grand Central or Penn? Why not indeed? At first the former was seriously contemplated. But then it was decided that the chances of being recognized by friends, business acquaintances, etc., at such a place, though remote, are greater than in some similar venue hundreds of miles away, and that the even remoter chance of being so recognized *in the act of depositing bottle* could nevertheless be fatal to the successful outcome of the experiment.

Further (and especially in the case of G.C.S.) : since one frequently uses that venue in the ordinary course of living, any unusual departure from one's regular behavior might well be noted by and arouse the curiosity of the official and semi-official habitués (e.g., redcaps, newsstand clerks, policemen).

And yet further the choice of such a place would immediately conflict with one's original precautionary guidelines, in this case the desirability of exploiting fully one's freedom of action in never conducting experiments in one's own neighborhood or general haunts. (See previous entry above.) Having business in the Cleveland area, therefore, and possessing a rough idea of venue as a result of an earlier visit, this was finally decided upon. It is a big station, frequented by bums, etc., busy enough to afford natural cover, yet not so busy (outside rush hours, one presumes) as to give one a *false* sense of security.

(b) The agent. Barbituric acid was chosen because one possessed already a good stock of sleeping pills, come by legally and naturally and without exciting any curiosity. This had the added advantage of making preliminary experiments (in the usual sense!) possible: i.e., testing for odor, flavor, coloration, solubility, etc. Furthermore, I was able to make sure, by the most discreet and unremarkable preliminary investigations, that the particular type of pill did not contain any built-in emetic—a most favorable augury indeed, if one cared to indulge in superstition when embarking on an undertaking of such, shall we say, life-and-death importance.

(c) The vehicle. Chosen as a result of experiments conducted in accordance with (b) above—and mainly, one might add, because of the opacity of most Scotch bottles. This would efficiently disguise the cloudiness and lightening of color imparted to the liquid by a high concentration of the drug. Since the type of subject chosen would be highly unlikely to drink his/her liquor from glass or cup, but would almost certainly drink straight from bottle (and probably bottle plus paper sack, at that), the look of the liquor would be irrelevant, given that opacity.

Further: It was found that the smell of the whisky was sufficiently strong to be retained in spite of the addition of the drug.

But why (always the queries!) only one third of a bottle? A good question. This was decided upon, after much thought, for two reasons:

(i) While your ordinary man in the street would certainly hesitate to drink from any unsealed, partially consumed bottle he might find, your wino has no such scruples, especially if the smell is right. On the other hand, while your ordinary man in the street might be tempted by an apparently untouched bottle, your wino—experienced in the matter of what is usually to be found in trash baskets, etc., and possessing a natural tendency to grossly overvalue the commodity—would probably be instantly suspicious. Fully intact fifths must very rarely, if ever, be thrown away like that. On the other hand, it must more than seldom occur that a secret tippler, or even a near-alcoholic, is moved to throw away the remains of a bottle—either to avoid detection on reaching home, or in a fit of remorse or determination to kick the habit.

(ii) A third of a bottle ensures a higher concentration of the draft—a more lethal mouthful, as it were.

4. *The Plan.* To proceed to the venue during the late morning, dressed low-keyed, quite normally (and being sure to wear gloves) and equipped with the preparation in a reasonably clean brown paper sack as if carrying a bottle for own consumption later. To circumambulate the venue not too casually, not too briskly, as if waiting for the arrival or departure of a train, noting the presence of bums, layabouts, etc., and any area they might appear to favor, and *quietly* alert for any too-curious observer. No loitering. No behavior likely to draw attention to oneself. Then to deposit in a litter basket, quickly and naturally, the bottle.

(Afterthought: to carry a few other articles—folded newspaper, another sack (sandwiches?), briefcase, and thereby avoid projecting, even subliminally, the image of A Man Carrying A Sack.)

REPORT ON EXPERIMENT

Initially at any rate: a fiasco, a shambles, a nightmare!

First, although the conditions seemed just right—fairly busy, not too many people around, not too few—would one believe I was not able to find, in the first circumambulation of that vast station, a single litter basket unattended?

A policeman stood by one of these receptacles—with his back to it, granted, but only two feet away. And a policeman . . .

A mother was persuading her little girl to be sick into another.

A bum with a beaver cap was busy bending over a third.

Two youths were playing a sort of tag around a fourth—constantly swinging on it, clutching its rim for support.

There may have been others quite free, of course, but by now I was considerably put out of my stride. I had to calm down. I had to take stock.

One thing was very obvious. There could be no quick breezing in and out, and maybe (I began to feel) that was to my advantage. It never pays to rush things in the early stages of an important new enterprise. And, after all, hadn't one of the obstacles been presented by a bum, doing exactly what was expected of him and thus confirming me in my choice of venue?

No. It was clear that I should have to settle for lingering—but a very casual, natural sort of lingering (hence my use of that word rather than "loitering"). Glancing at my watch, looking up at the indicators. There was no danger of attracting attention, let alone courting suspicion, in that, I decided. Not when one is so very respectably attired, so very ordinary.

But then: what *is* ordinary? And if one is the only ordinary person in a certain place—?

I soon had to start revising my ideas along such lines.

"Are you thinking what I'm thinking, sir, yes you are I can see it in your face . . ."

All in one breath, like that. A big man, big rosy dewlaps, tufted gray eyebrows, little piggy eyes, touching my arm, only a half-inch away from the neck of the bottle nestling in the sack. Well dressed, also very respectable, ordinary.

"Huh?" I grunted, but politely, only grunting because I'd warned myself earlier to avoid attracting attention to my accent.

He stabbed a pigskin finger, pig in pigskin, toward the two boys still larking around the trash bin. I felt myself begin to redden. I hadn't been aware of it until he pointed it out, but I had been staring at them—or, rather, at it.

"Damn near knocked that lady off her feet, and you know what I'd do, I'd draft the both of 'em, that's what!"

"Hnng!" I grunted, not wanting to start any argument on any subject with anyone. But grunting still, it will be observed, still wary, warier than ever about the accent. His hand was off my arm, but it had brushed the edge of the sack.

"Yeah, I know, I know," he muttered, continuing to glare (but at them, I was glad to note, not me—for I was only a pair of ears to him, and glad to remain so), "I know you're thinking they're too young, what—thirteen? fourteen?—but in that case why the hell aren't they in school? Hah? No. Draft 'em, and all brats like them, soon settle the inner urban delinquency problems. *And* send 'em out operationally, Christ, they're old enough, some of the best goon infantry in Vietnam, both sides, kids that age, younger, yeah."

That was only one.

I was no sooner free of him and over at the other end of the concourse, glancing at my watch, looking up at the indicators, than I was accosted by a little old woman in black: black coat, black stockings, black hat—and all a throwback to the forties, with the hat of the Robin Hood type, tilted forward, and the coat with high, wide padded shoulders.

"Excuse me, are *you* Jim?"

"Mngmm?" I grunted.

"No, I guess you're not." She was looking up at me very intently, eyes doing a minute square-by-square survey of my face. Just the way I had hoped *not* to be looked at.

"But then," she said, looking all of a sudden into a certain square, possibly my chin, or the right-hand corner of my mouth, "you must have changed some this last twenty-seven years, of *course* you're Jim!"

"No, I'm sorry, ma'am," I said, risking it, but taking care to Americanize my accent. "My name is Trevor."

She started back, looking shocked—but indignant shocked, just as if I'd been trying to get fresh with her, the old fool.

Then she said, "Oh . . . well," and hurried off.

I needed a drink myself by now. I saw a cocktail lounge nearby and went straight in. Like the rest of the place, it was busy enough but not too busy. Safe, I thought—and really I did require a place to sit and take stock.

Would I have to abandon the experiment? Had I already sufficiently imprinted my image on the memories of two people? Or would they be likely to discard it almost immediately, allowing it to be crowded out by the pressures of their own obsessions?

"Hi! You're Virgo, aren't you?"

It was a waitress. Blonde, thin, sallow, fortyish-hovering, her nameplate fixed sloppily, upside down, but turning out to be *Mona*.

I was wondering how to answer, and whether a case of mistaken identity clinched it or eased the situation. A big laugh might ensue if this Virgo character should be cited as the depositor of the fatal bottle. . . .

"I can always tell a Virgo," she said, prattling on. "The minute you came in, the way you headed straight for this table, he's a Virgo, I said."

Now I understood. I cleared my throat, set my nasal muscles, and once more faked an accent.

"I'm not interested in astrology," I said coolly, "but I wouldn't mind a Sc—" I must have gulped a little, pulling up in time, "a bourbon on the rocks."

"Scotch—bourbon. Now what's it gonna be? *That* isn't the way a Virgo orders."

I told her bourbon and looked away. It did the trick and she went.

When she returned with the drink, she said:

"Know what? You're the first person in here today not interested in astrology. I always take a guess at their sign—and nine out of ten I'm right—and they're always interested, even the tenth."

She was looking at the stuff I had deposited on the table—the folded newspaper, the sandwich sack—and then in one continuous curve at the stuff on the chair at the side of me—the briefcase, the other sack, upright against the chairback.

Then she sniffed. Exactly as if that last item explained everything.

I gave the experiment one last chance. After a semi-circumambulation, I sat on a bench, my eye mentally if not actually on the litter bin near which the policeman had been standing. He wasn't there now, but I wished to find out just where he'd moved to. Then someone behind, sitting back to back with me on another bench—it developed into some ghastly kind of love-seat situation, I couldn't help thinking later—leaned his head back and whispered hoarsely:

"Y' got a quarter to spare, mister?"

If it wasn't the bum in the beaver hat! Or someone remarkably like him. It was uncanny. And his breath stank. And his head remained near mine, turned to mine. And I was petrified.

Had I not been, I should have hurried to give him a quarter, or simply got up and walked away.

"Huh!" he blasted, in the same stinking abrasive whisper. "Too high and mighty, huh? Well, listen, you. I got your number, mister. I know your sort. I know whatcher got in that sack!"

I nearly swooned. *Was* I dreaming? Was I still back in the motel?

"Hey, friend"—more wheedling now—"no offense, huh? How about just a slug of medicine, huh, for a fellow sufferer, huh? Come on, George"—sneering now—"pass the poison, why doncha?"

He actually said *that*.

And now, when I opened my eyes, I saw the cop was back by the trash can. Maybe he'd never left. I didn't know. I didn't know anything. And he was looking straight at me. Or seemed to be.

I got up. Mission abandoned, thinking who would have thought it could be so difficult.

Out in the streets I half considered making my way to some public gardens I had noticed previously, a place with a view over the Indians' stadium and the lake. No doubt there were trash bins and bums up there. But I decided against it. The experiment had been a flop. It seemed to me that the whole project required careful re-thinking. Yet—such is the tenacity of the truly scientific mind—it just didn't occur to me simply to stuff the sack into some bin on the street on the way to the parking garage and forget it.

In the light of subsequent events, that was most fortunate.

Her Journal:
Entry Number 4

Now *that*, if you'll pardon my interruption, explains what had been quite a big mystery for yours truly, whatever else it does. About the sleeping pills, I mean. I always did think there was something fishy about them, well now I know.

You see during that summer when he'd been—well *we'd* been—getting all nervy, it affected him so he couldn't get off to sleep so well some nights. It didn't affect me the same, I suppose it's psychological, when you know you don't have to get up for a certain time in the morning it doesn't matter you not dropping off so soon. But Ron, it made it worse for him and honestly it got so that I thought we'd have to split up, I mean at nights, to sleep in different rooms not just different beds.

Anyway I persuaded him to get some pills from the doctor. He didn't want to at first, hates drugs of any kind, says, "I like to be my own man, no matter what"—nothing religious, you understand, just Ron, just—well—pigheaded is one thing I can think of calling it.

Anyway, as I say, it got so that he went in the end and got the pills, fifty or sixty of them I think, I didn't like prying, it was enough to have got him to go to the doctor, and if I'd gone on nagging he might have flared, thinking I was getting the upper hand as he once called it when he was in bed with influenza nearly pneumonia. So I kept quiet, but honestly, I began to wonder, because if he was taking them they weren't having much effect, toss toss, turn turn, nearly every night. And then I had a look, on the Q.T., and saw that if he was taking them it was just every once in a while, because the bottle was still nearly full, and then I began to study him a bit closer and I saw that this was so, one night every three seemed to be about it.

So that was that and in a bit I forgot all about it until the vacation and when I was packing I nearly forgot and said, "Oh I mustn't forget your sleeping pills, Ron," and I opened the drawer he kept them in, with his handkerchiefs, and he said, "No, don't bother, I've got so that I can manage without them altogether," and true enough, there was the bottle three quarters full, so I left them where they were.

Now remember that, three quarters full, because I did, I remembered that all right, about a week after we'd got back, it couldn't have been more, and I was putting some fresh handkerchiefs in his drawer and there the bottle was, empty but for two—just two—pills.

So "Hello!" I thought. "Don't tell me he's been taking two or three or four every night, which he must have, this rate." And, what with that being a *very* sticky period, as I mentioned before or as Ron would say "above" (why does he put "above" always when he means way back, many pages?)—anyway what with things being that way I got quite a scare, thinking: "Oh *no!* Is he hoarding them up, is he thinking of Ending It All, is it that bad?"

But then I got to thinking, "Don't be silly, Pat, why should he bother to take them out of that bottle and hoard them somewhere else?" And in the end I decided he must have taken some with him to Canada after all, and had been taking them every night since getting home, and not saying, not wanting to admit that he had to depend on them. And that was so like our Ronald that I felt satisfied straight away and even thanked my lucky stars I hadn't mentioned it because then he *would* have been annoyed, I kid you not!

But now of course I can see exactly what was behind it.

Well!

Well now don't get me wrong, don't think I believe all this about the Big Experiment, you joking? No. But knowing Ron I certainly do believe all about the theories—theories, that's Ron all right—and about the *little* experiments, the preliminaries. That's Ron again all right. I can just see him down in the basement or locked up in the bathroom testing those pills for—what did he say?—oh yes, for odor, flavor, color, solubility, and that. Like a schoolkid, sometimes I think a good present for him for Christmas would be one of those chemistry sets.

No but I mean. Once you get past those preliminaries, all that Venue, Agent, Vehicle, Notes stuff and get down to the nitty gritty, can't you see the difference? Or is it just me, knowing Ron the way I do? I mean that business on Cleveland Station. Typical Ron, a typical Ronald tale, he loves to tell them, all deadpan, never smiles, even looks hurt when you laugh, it makes it even funnier. I sometimes think I'll die laughing when Ron's in one of his tale-telling moods. Once my father nearly choked when we were courting, one Sunday teatime, and Ron was telling us about his driver's test which he failed. Poor Dad, he was purple in the face till he coughed up the chunk of boiled ham that went down the wrong way with laughing. And all Ron could say afterward, still deadpan, just to me, when you'd think he might have relaxed, was, "Serve him damn well right if he had choked, it wasn't funny being failed for something as stupid as *that!*"

Yes. Well. Same with this. Yet not *just* the same. First time round, reading it yesterday, and it was one of the bits I picked out first because it had more talking in it, people talking, and not so many long words, that first time round when I read it I laughed out loud.

But then when I read the next, because don't worry, he hasn't finished with that story yet, I didn't laugh so much, because say what you like, even if he was making it up, only wishing he'd done it, only playing with the idea, which I think is what it was, well even so he is sick, poor soul, he must be.

Just listen to, I mean just read this next bit and see what you think *then.*

His Journal:
Entry Number 2 (continued)

Fortunate also was the fact that I had already accomplished my business—my normal business—in Cleveland. After the fiasco, I wanted nothing more than to get away from the place, fast. It was almost a feeling of panic I had; a sense of flight, stronger even than if I had done what I'd set out to do, because this was flight from myself, from a realization of failure, and failure after so many fine hopes, brave words, bold plans.

How I intended to try and recoup, or even *if* I intended to try and recoup, I am still not sure. Somewhere at the back of my mind I suppose I had a vague idea of making the attempt on the way back, at Buffalo, say, or Rochester. I had no more calls to make, it was Friday, I was not due back in the office until Monday, I could always telephone my wife to say I had been unavoidably delayed and wouldn't be home until Sunday. But then again, also at the back of my mind, there must have lurked another idea, shadow to the first, that I did not know the main station at either of those places, and that if I could not manage it at a venue I did know reasonably well, what would be my chances at these others? And what the extra risks?

At the moment, however, all I wanted was to put as much mileage between myself and Cleveland as possible, and, since it was a clear dry sunny afternoon, it wasn't long before I'd put the state as well as the city far behind me, and not only that state but the next. In short, I was across the Pennsylvania border and speeding along the New York Thruway not long after three—with "speeding" the opera-

tive word. Indeed, when the highway patrol passed me at 3:15 I felt
sure that it would be to flag me down, and then I did feel panic.

Not because of the prospect of being booked for that offense, it
must be understood. I had led a pretty charmed life in that respect
since coming to the States. For an Englishman *not* to be booked
for speeding under the sweeping influence of the euphoria, the sense
of release, at suddenly, after years of narrow-gutted British rabbit
runs, finding himself in a fast car on excellent roads, is something
remarkable, and in fact I had escaped my just deserts for almost exactly twelve months now. No. What caused the panic was my suddenly remembering the bottle.

By this time it had quite gone out of my mind. The clear afternoon, blue sky, mellow sunlight had all combined to remind me of an
earlier trip in the vicinity, on the parallel route nearer the shore of
the lake, itself narrower and more twisting but still a prince to most
British so-called A roads, and enhanced then (late August, just before the vacation) by roadside farmers' produce stalls piled with the
early fruits of the harvest.

A soothing memory—and then the patrol car. And all at once I
remembered the bottle, and with it another memory, or half-memory.
Wasn't there some kind of law about carrying liquor on the Thruway? And there it was, still in its sack, wedged on the back seat with
the untouched sandwiches and unread newspaper next to my briefcase. Christ. An unsealed, seemingly partly consumed bottle of seeming whisky. No use protesting:

"No, no, officer. That's not *really* whisky. Or at least not in the
condition you are probably thinking of. No question of intoxication,
you understand. No question of even *tasting* it myself. One sip and
I'd be out. Two and I'd be dead. Here, try it."

As I say, no use protesting that version of my innocence.

But then, to my relief, the patrol continued in the fast lane without flagging me down, and for the time being I was safe. Nevertheless, my nerves were all alive to the danger now—remote though it
really was, for I was careful to keep within the limit from that point
on—and I decided to leave the Thruway at the next opportunity. I
still didn't know whether I was going to abandon the experiment
entirely, or embark on a makeshift somewhere, but it struck me that
I had better do my deciding under less hazardous circumstances.

So I left at the next interchange and headed southwest, and I
couldn't have made a better (and I mean that in the positive sense)

move had I been planning it for months. For it was not only a question of geography, as it turned out, but also of timing. Five minutes earlier or five minutes later—but especially five minutes earlier, one must be exact in these things—and the opportunity would never have presented itself.

However, that is to anticipate. Suffice it to say that it wasn't more than an hour after I had left the Thruway, meandering and musing along a quiet stretch of country road in the general direction of Route 17, which I had decided to take as an alternative, when I saw him. Or, rather, it. The yellow Plymouth that seemed to me at first to be so incongruous in this part of the country (for a moment I thought it was a New York cab).

It had been parked outside one of those dim shacks that pass for bars in these places. And it swung out into the road ahead of me—not many yards ahead of me, I might add—in such a way that it wasn't hard to guess that it had been parked there for some considerable time. It was, as I say, a quiet road. There was nothing behind me, nothing to bash into me unavoidably as I equally unavoidably braked, but it was obviously all the same to the driver of the Plymouth. Still thinking in terms of New York cabs, I suppose, I gave him a blast of the horn, to which he responded by raising a finger and swerving in such a manner as to churn up a quantity of dust at the side of the pavement. Then he accelerated in a thicker cloud and pulled ahead.

I let him. I was in no mood to accept any challenges. On the contrary. Noting his continued manner of driving, I was beginning to regret having given him the original blast. Tangling with some drunken redneck was the last thing I wanted.

But he swept away around the bend, and when I saw him again the yellow splash was considerably smaller, and I was just settling down to think about more important matters when I noticed that he'd cut across the highway diagonally and disappeared behind some trees.

This gave me pause.

Clearly he'd not made a left turn. There was no appreciable slowing, certainly no indication, no sharp angle, and no junction sign. But then I saw the picnic-area sign and realized that that must have been where he'd gone. I slowed down while I reflected. There wasn't another car in sight and probably the picnic spot would be deserted at that time of the day. Was the fool planning some drunken stunt? Another sudden swoop into the road ahead of me? Or worse —some direct attempt at ramming? Was the blasting I'd given him continuing to rankle?

As I approached the area I decided to take no chances. I would suddenly accelerate and sweep past faster than he anticipated. To stay as slow as I was was asking for trouble. So I did. I put my foot down hard, keeping a wary eye cocked to the left. And there, sure enough, was the Plymouth, its nose tilted ready toward the road, ready to—

But no. Fast as I was passing, I was still able to see that there was no danger of interception from that quarter. Such may have been the man's intention, I don't know, but as of now he was going nowhere in a hurry. Over my shoulder I took it in at a glance: the splintered bench, the uptilted picnic table, the buckled fender, the bloodstained forehead leaning out of the window.

Instinctively, I pulled up. It was a fairly long area and I turned into a bay about a hundred yards farther along. He had seemed to be conscious. I had seen his head turn and lift a little as I passed. It didn't even occur to me that this might be a ruse to decoy me out of the car; and equally I am able to swear that I had no thought in my mind other than to give whatever help I could. I ran to the Plymouth.

"You all right?" I asked.

He was still sitting there, leaning out, with the blood dripping slowly from the gash above his right eye. His head lurched up. He was an older man than I had imagined, with thick but close-cropped iron-gray hair. His eyes were of the protruding kind, a fact that was obvious even though they were almost shut, concealed by layer upon layer of lizardlike flesh.

"You fergoff!" he said, like that, drawling it, trying to open his eyes, to glare, to sneer, then: "Wow!" he groaned, the pose crumpling as his head lurched again. "Hoo!" he went, putting a hand to the side of his head.

"You want to climb out?" I asked, still anxious for a fellow human being's safety, drunk or not—a purely natural reflex.

"You wanner get—?" he began, perking aggressively again. Then: "Hoo!" again. And: "Wow!"—as he tried working his jaw. "Yuh— say . . ." He blinked. "You wouldn't have—hoo—a drink, would you?"

Judging from the smell of his breath, he should have had enough inside him to withstand the shock of a dozen collisions. Then I remembered.

I looked around. Deserted.

"I'll be right back," I said.

It was safe enough, I told myself, as I hurried to the car. Of course it was. If any other motorist stopped, I needn't deliver it. I had right up until the last possible moment to snatch it back, to say, "No, second thoughts, you've had enough, buster," and to say to any newcomer, "He's had enough, I've just realized."

And what an opportunity. So much better than back there. Why now, I told myself, as I snatched my gloves from the passenger seat and then took up the bottle from the back—now I can give it a shake. Seconds before he puts it to his lips, less than seconds, I can give it a good shake.

I had been having misgivings about the sedimentation earlier in the day. I had tried to rationalize them away, counting on things like the angle of tilt an eager wino would give it, and the suction factor of a parched throat, tongue, lips. But this was all taken care of now.

Shaking the bottle already, I ran back to the Plymouth.

"Do you have a glass or anything?" I asked, a little too carried away by my over-anxiety, knowing it would spoil my chances of a successful outcome if he had.

"Huh?"

He was peering at the bottle. Doubtfully?

"A glass?" I said, looking round, listening for the sounds of any approaching engine.

"Wass in there, Scotch?"

"Yes."

"You wouldn' have any vodka, wouldya?"

Maybe it was as well, I began to think, sensing a further cruel twist in the terrible luck I seemed to have been stuck with that day.

"Sorry," I said.

"Argh, what th' hell!" he groaned, reaching out. "Gimme."

He took the cork off himself.

I watched as he tilted the bottle, watched his throat, streaked with already congealing blood, work once, twice, three times, as he gulped.

"Wow!"

He seemed to gag as he wrenched the bottle away.

"Jeez! Never—never did—jeez—Scotch?"

I tried to speak, couldn't, nodded instead.

"Never did like the stuff, wow . . . you . . . you . . . ?"

He was motioning toward me with the bottle.

"No. I've had all I want," I said. "You just stay there now." I began to back away. "Take it easy, just take it easy . . ." His face was beginning to twitch, to bunch, to crack, to swell. "Just try to sleep," I said. "I'll go get . . ."

Purposely, I let it hang there.

As I hurried back to the car, I thought I heard a croaking kind of cry. I glanced back, but he seemed to have slumped already. I turned just once more before moving out of sight, into the bay where I'd left the car, and was a little surprised, but gratified, to see that he'd rallied sufficiently to be tilting the bottle again.

Then, taking care to drive out in such a way that he'd have no chance to see the number with even the clearest, most sober eyes in the world, I left him there.

My heart continued to thump for another ten miles or so. But, as may be imagined, I was happy, deeply satisfied, fulfilled. For how much better, how infinitely better, a victim of that kind than some mere derelict! How better that it should be a man who was obviously most reckless of the lives of others, not just any drunk, but a chronic drunk, he had to be, drunk drivers always are. In short, a man whose death—and what the hell, he looked sixty if he was a day—might well save the lives of others, true innocents, whose only crime was to be on the road (or at the side of it, supposing it had been summer, kids picnicking?) at the same time and in the same place as he.

Such were my feelings that afternoon and evening, as I drove home—back on the Thruway again, no worries now, mission accomplished. But such too is the nature of Success—and it had never been brought home to me so forcibly before—that one is rarely if every allowed to savor it to the full. Circumstances, it seems, are always ready to conspire to dilute it, to spread it thin. Always there is the need for confirmation, and almost never does it coincide with the triumphant moment itself. Life seems forever to insist on photo finishes, which need processing, which takes time. Hence the delayed ratification, the complicated proviso, the wait for the check that is supposed to be paid on signature of a contract, the Escrow Factor.

Naturally, I continued to feel pleased. Naturally, I went around feeling quietly happy for days. But always these feelings were accompanied by a vague uneasiness, which gradually deepened as I drew blanks in the newspapers—not just the New York papers, but also the out-of-town prints I bought regularly and religiously at that stand specializing in them: *The Plain Dealer*, the *Buffalo Courier-Express*, even the *Erie News*, and one or two more. And I was beginning to despair of ever gaining confirmation of the result when finally—more than a week later!—I came upon the following news item, appropriately enough just in time for Thanksgiving.

REST-AREA DEATH MYSTERY SOLVED

Wesburg, N.Y., Monday—The body of the man found in a highway rest area on a quiet scenic route six miles south of Wesburg ten days ago has now been positively identified by the deceased's widow. The dead man was Otis P. Newstrander, 57, an insurance assessor, of Harrisburg, Pa. Giving evidence at the resumed inquest here today, Mrs. Annette Newstrander said that although her husband had experienced business and domestic worries during the past four years, he had never threatened to take his life. "I just cannot understand it," she said, when questioned by the coroner, Dr. Elliot Worsthorne. "Although he was a heavy drinker and this had been the cause of most of our problems, his attitude was always aggressive, sometimes violent, never remorseful. No history of depression at all." Questioned further, she admitted that as a result of an argument the previous week, she had left home on an extended visit to friends in Baltimore. She had left no forwarding address and this was the reason for the delay in tracing her. "But this leaving home for a week or two was something that happened regularly, at least once a year. It could not have been the cause for depression even if he had been the type."

Witness Breaks Down

Regarding the location, she stated that she had to agree with an earlier witness in that as far as she knew, her husband had no business connections in the area at all. "I can only figure that he might have been looking for me." Asked why, she explained that their honeymoon and some of the happiest vacations in the early years of the marriage had been spent in the Niagara–Erie vicinity. At this point the witness broke down.

Resuming evidence after a brief adjournment, the witness said that her husband had never had any insomnia problem and she had no idea where he might have obtained the pills. Although she herself was a poor sleeper, she had never taken such medications, nor did she believe in doing so. "But I will say this," she added. "I find it very strange he should have taken them with whisky, a drink he very rarely touched. Vodka, yes. That was his favorite. Or gin."

Coroner's Summary

Summarizing, the coroner touched on this point, observing that it was not at all unlikely that a heavy drinker with a marked preference for one type of liquor should choose for such a purpose one he liked less. Then, moving on to that purpose, the coroner said he felt there could be no doubt about the intention of the deceased. "He had taken a sufficient quantity of barbiturates to kill himself several times over. We have heard evidence that he had been drinking heavily, alone, that afternoon, and that his mood was noticeably uncommunicative, to the point of surliness in fact. As if, in the words of one witness, 'He had a big load of trouble on his mind and wasn't happy about it.' The cuts and abrasions sustained in the collision with the picnic table were minor and could be dismissed as in any way contributing toward his death."

The verdict was given as death from an overdose of barbiturates, self-administered while the balance of mind was disturbed. A rider was added to the effect that although prompt medical attention might have saved the deceased's life, no blame could be attached to the local farmer who stated in evidence at the earlier hearing that he had gone to investigate the Plymouth on the afternoon in question and had concluded that the man inside was sleeping off the effects of drink.

Widow Not Satisfied

In an interview later, the widow said that she was not satisfied with the verdict. "Otis was no angel, but he would never take his own life, I am convinced. Not even on the spur of the moment, and this took time to prepare, obviously." Asked if she had any other theory, she replied, "All I can say is that someone else must have administered it or tricked him into it. As I said in evidence, he did have business worries—who doesn't?—but in his business it is usually the other guy who has bigger worries." Asked to elucidate, she said that while she knew her husband had made enemies in the course of his work, he never named names. "But it could be that this time he uncovered something really big, maybe Syndicate shenanigans, and if so I aim to find out." When contacted by your reporter, a spokesman for Midwest & Penn. Insurance, Mr. Newstrander's employers, dismissed this as "nonsense," adding: "With all due respect to the widow, for whom we have the deepest sympathy, this sounds like the typical reaction of an overwrought mind."

The police here refused to comment on Mrs. Newstrander's statement beyond this: "As far as we are concerned, the case is now off our books."

Her Journal:
   Entry Number 5

I don't mind telling you I had a little cry while I was copying that down, poor woman, and if I thought for one moment that Ron really had done this thing, I would
   Well?
   What?
   What *would* you do, Pat?
   Oh I don't know what, I'm getting so I don't know what to think, but of course he didn't do any such thing so why fret? Personally I wouldn't mind betting there was a lot more than meets the eye in what she said about the Syndicate and if I was her I think I might have been a bit more careful about what I said to that reporter, you never know. No, though. All *Ron* did was find this bit in the paper, must have taken his fancy, maybe with having been there himself, in that area at the same time, maybe passing the same spot. Then he would start working backward, nothing to stop him, and inventing all the rest, he was damned careful to leave out the dates you'll notice. But even so, as I say, just that itself is a very sick thing to do and you can't help worrying.
   Anyway, it solves another little mystery. All those out-of-town papers he keeps coming home with from time to time. *He* says it helps in his business, to know all the local news of a place when he goes to visit people there, they much appreciate it, he says, makes a good impression, and I must say it's the sort of thing he *would* think of, Mr. Thorough, like that time we were courting and he read up

all that stuff about my father's job, a printer, and spouted it back at him. But what I never could understand about these newspapers was why he mostly took them *after* he'd been there on a trip and wouldn't be going again maybe for months. But then I put it down to some kind of follow-up system, I don't know, it's hard to follow *him*, the way he thinks, I just give up. But now of course I *can* see why. Now it figures. If

Hold on, Pat. Wait. Whoa. What *are* you saying, girl? It only figures if he actually *did* do these things. I mean.

Oh the hell with it. I'm tired. It's late. You're just going round in circles.

So all right. I'll leave it now. There's a lot to report about what he was like at home after that trip, especially the Thanksgiving that year, so I'd better get my beauty sleep and be fresh and alert to tackle it in the morning.

Her Journal:
Entry Number 6

At first I thought it was a woman.

Yes, thinking back, concentrating (as soon as I was awake this morning I was concentrating, because there's not all that much time left, Thursday already, hell) I remembered.

I thought it was a woman.

Had to be.

I mean the signs were all there.

Like one. He kept looking in the mirror. Even when he came in and he kissed me in the hall I caught him glancing over my shoulder, looking at himself, and I remember thinking then, well that's not like Ron, only when he's sick sometimes, and somehow he did look, well, I suppose you might call it feverish—glittery eyes, with those two red spots of color just underneath the eyes—so I kept my own eyes on him. But no, it wasn't a fever, and yes, even when the glitter had gone and he was normal color, sallowish though don't tell him I said it, even then and for days and days after, weeks, he never has really broken off the habit, I'd catch him at it. Mirrors, store windows, ordinary windows so long as they showed a reflection, even a knife once, a table knife, waiting for supper, there he was with it up in front of his face and across, must have been his eyes he was looking at, but it gave me such a turn I nearly dropped the casserole I was bringing in.

Like two. The change in his whatsit, attitude, general damn what's the word, but you know. He seemed—well he *was*, I suppose, he's not one for disguising his feelings generally, not for any length of time that is—happier. Happier in a quiet sort of way. Calmer. More content. Less touchy.

Which really counts three. Not just less touchy in a vague sort of way, I don't mean that. I mean being less touchy in a way I never would have dreamed he would be less touchy, before that trip to Cleveland. Being less touchy about the things that really had got on his wires, and deeper than that even, and what I mean is less touchy about Palmers Rotten Point, the neighbors, and even Charlie Raybourn.

And now four, and I mean this should rate four five and six, because believe me, to me this seemed the clincher. Because it was then, just after he'd got back from that trip, that he started wearing jockey shorts. All his life he'd been wearing those things, trunks, those baggy ones, all his married life anyway, and a year or two before that, and could I get him to change (I mean he looked so ridiculous sometimes, long thin spidery hairy legs, they would have looked so much better, well they did, they do, with this other style), could I the devil. But now, just like that, without saying a word, he went and bought himself eight pairs one day that week and that was that.

Oh yes, my lad, I thought. It's a woman or I'm a Dutchman. And well—now I feel a bit, well a bit mean, being so definite about it, jumping to conclusions, or *hopping* to them, it, one two three four, like that. But after all it was only natural. Especially after a year in this place, remember. I mean that's their biggest headache, the women here, they're always talking about it, afternoons especially, whenever there's a few get together, and it's always the same. What it's like in New York regarding women. They were always on about it, telling me about it, and they still are, and do, and after a bit it gets under your skin, you stop smiling to yourself and thinking, Silly bitches, nothing else to worry about—and you start worrying yourself. You know. About all the temptations their husbands are going through, and how some fall and some don't.

I mean honestly you'd never believe it. I mean women in England, well I suppose anywhere—but here it is something else again. Maybe it's with New York being so concentrated, everyone on top of everyone else (now! now!) but you know what I mean. So it gets to be a bee in their bonnet, the wives on the outskirts, waiting every day for it to happen and wondering if it already has and how can the bastard put up such a good performance, yes, getting to think *that* even if there's not the slightest scrap of evidence. I mean it's laughable really, I used to listen to them and take it all in, but afterward I had to laugh. Ron and I had many a good laugh about it in fact, especially at first, when we were still in a laughing mood as you might say.

"What makes it worse for them," he used to say, "is that they've deliberately chosen to stay out of it. They've instinctively drawn back, cold feet, frightened of all that close competition, not wanting to be seen at a disadvantage."

"Well I hope you don't think I've got cold feet," I used to say, just to hear him reply, all fierce and flashing:

"Don't be stupid!"

Well now it looked as if there might be something in it, and I got to wondering what she might be like, and what was the connection with the Cleveland trip, and I came to the conclusion that—

But hold it. You see? *Conclusion.* Get it?

I really had got it as bad as some of these bitches.

They all had conclusions too. Theories, they made them sound like, but if you thought about it (Ron put me wise to this himself, who else?) you soon came to see that they were really conclusions. Based on what they *thought* they knew about New York and what they certainly *did* know about their husbands.

For example. (No. I owe him this. I have to spell it out. Take your medicine, Pat.)

For example.

With Sylvia Raybourn it was secretaries. No other kind of girls or women. Just secretaries. With lots of other wives here it was the same, I know, and I suppose there's always something in it, just the fact that these kids are young. I mean let's face it, they've got youth on their side (or should I say their front, high up, and on their back, low down, still in good shape, you get it?) but that's only understandable, and I must say it never bothered me. Although, touch wood, I suppose I am a bit unusual keeping my figure the way I have (another reason why the bitches are always dropping hints about how sorry they are for childless couples).

Anyway. Where was I? Oh yes. Sylvia. Well with her it wasn't just secretaries (she's the dumpy sort by the way, nice neat little face and neck and lovely natural blond hair, *still* natural I'm sure, but her figure spreading like a Christmas tree from there on down to the bottom of her skirt). No. With her, all this Charlie-bait was Secretaries Plus. She had a theory that all these big corporations, including Eastern Seals of course, always had a certain number of call girls posing as secretaries. Charlie had once told her about one corporation (*not* Eastern Seals) doing this, as extra inducements for big clients, and she thought about it and thought about it until she'd reduced it to a general New York practice, only inducements for higher executives, not just clients.

May Zetlinger once told me on the Q.T. that she looked on this as evidence of Sylvia's terrific vanity ("*Dumb* vanity, of course, dear!") in thinking she (Sylvia) would be more than a match for any teenage kid, but just couldn't do anything against such professional competition.

May herself is just a secretary woman. I mean that's what she worries about—just straightforward ordinary girl secretaries. She's got a pretty good figure left to say she's had six kids, and she can still wear clothes made for girls a quarter of a century less and wear them well, but she's lost her juices, she doesn't mind admitting.

"No. If *that* kind of Super-Secretary was all I had to worry about where Harry's concerned I'd be happy enough."

"And she can say that again!" said Julia Piscola, when I happened to mention it. "So long as they're young is good enough for Harry Zetlinger. You'd think with so many kids of his own he'd have a thing going for the Older Woman, but no, not Mister Zetlita—sorry—Zetlinger."

As for Julia, *she* has a theory about it was the bosses' wives who were the biggest danger in New York. "Sugar Mommas," she calls them. "*They* don't live out of town, you notice. Not during the week they don't."

And maybe, as some said, this took root in her head because Gene Piscola was the tall tight-lipped military type who only seemed to unbend with older women, and then some, being very gallant about it. I mean gallant the way they are in old movies, Viennese ballroom type, click-click, kiss-hand, very correct but kind of flowery, and very nice when you're on the receiving end but kind of shivery, know what I mean?

Then—but why go on? With some it was women bosses themselves (Muriel Adams was one of these, mainly I think because Mort is in cosmetics and three of the top executives are women in his corporation), and with some (well, one, I'm thinking of Brenda Hunter now) it is the call girls themselves and the prostitutes, not playing at being secretaries or anything like that but in their own right, hanging about in droves, in hordes according to her, outside the office buildings every afternoon from four thirty on, lining the routes to Grand Central and Penn Stations, especially black prostitutes who she says no white man can resist no matter what they say, and with others it wasn't pros or secretaries or bosses or bosses' wives but all the career girls, bachelor girls, and particularly the Jewish ones who, to hear some of these wives talk, are even deadlier than the black pros are to poor little homely dowdy Brenda Hunter.

So. That's Palmers Point, and a place where all that's brewing day after day, afternoon after afternoon, can get pretty poisonous, pretty polluted, yes, Palmers Point, wasn't there a famous poisoner, Palmer, well I don't suppose it was named after him, but it might just as well have been.

So.

So anyway, laugh though I had, it must have worked its way into my veins, this poison, because with this change in Ron I wasn't laughing any more and I started to get my own theory and you know what it was?

For some reason I started suspecting that with him it was a college girl, or maybe a drop-out but clever, yes, maybe one of these clever drop-outs but clean (she'd have to be that for Ron), yes, either a college girl on her way back to Columbia or some gorgeous but clean hippie making her way to Greenwich Village. Who he'd given a lift to on the way back, making sparkling conversation (nothing more at first, Ron being slow but sure) all the way from Cleveland to the Tappan Zee Bridge.

So I started keeping my eyes and ears open, and my nostrils too (but naturally), just mild snooping you might say, nothing very serious (telling myself nothing would come of it, no follow-up), and I had to admit that if they were meeting in New York it would have to be lunchtimes, because he was always back on the same train, 5:53 at Palmers Point, though of course a lot could be done lunchtimes with someone who had an apartment handy or should I say pad.

And I might have stopped suspecting by the end of the first week, and certainly the second, because there was so little to go on, if it hadn't been for two more changes I began to notice.

Like one. Changing his drink without any reason. From Scotch and water to vodka martinis, which struck me as being a bit of a smart-ass kind of drink, just the sort you might change to if you'd started messing around with a gorgeous rich heiress-type hippie. (Though not straight college girl, I had to admit. No. Someone sophisticated it had to be, and there were times when I began to veer to the bachelor-girl theory, maybe someone he'd met in New York just before the trip and had taken her with him. The things you think!)

And two, another clincher. He started using after-shave lotion and deodorant. Ron. My Ron, who when I'd once bought him some after-shave for Christmas back in England said, "Sorry, Pat, but you don't catch *me* going around smelling like some pox-doctor's clerk!" Old Ron who'd always said it was a racket this male-cosmetics thing ("Ask Mort Adams!") and there was nothing it could do that plain soap and water couldn't.

I tell you I might have started getting *very* broody about the lunchtime-apartment theory. But what seemed to rule all my suspicions out, or at least keep me from losing my cool, was his behavior with me in bed, if you can call it *in* bed, some of the things he started. I mean right from getting back, from that first kiss in the hall (when he looked at himself), he was all over me. Every night it was the same, and that was unusual, because

Anyway, that's our business.

All I'm saying is that there were these changes and that although it looked very much as if it might be another woman at first, when you come to think about it more closely it looked as if it really couldn't have been. So after a bit I began to decide that it must be something entirely different, something to do with work, and when the Raybourns invited us to the Thanksgiving Party it looked as if I might have hit on it.

Because, you see, the way things had been going during the past six months, that invitation simply was not *on*. I mean I think I've said enough to prove that. I mean we weren't exactly daggers drawn, but things had been getting very chilly, so chilly that Sylvia hadn't bothered to turn her smile on when we met at the supermarket or wherever.

But now—all change. Here we were invited. Cordially. With bells on. So sudden. And all at once I thought I had it.

"Ha!" I said to myself. "Things are looking up at work. Old Ron Fox must have pulled off something pretty big, some pretty big contract, that trip upstate and Cleveland. Now I wonder why he hasn't been bragging about it to me already?"

But I didn't wonder for long. I mean you get to know how things are when you reach my age (listen to Grandma!). No but you get to know you never can be sure of anything until it's in the bag, not absolutely sure, and these business things always take time, two or three weeks, often more (it's right what he put about Success back there, you have to admit). Anyway it's what crossed my mind at the time.

So.

The party.

Talk about a comeback! It

(Good God I've just seen the time. Another whole morning gone already. But the party's important. Now I see that, anyway, and I just know it can't be skipped. So I'll snatch a bite of lunch and then continue.)

Her Journal:
Entry Number 7

Did I say important?

God, I didn't know just *how* important. Not until it suddenly came to me over lunch and I nearly bit my tongue off.

Because by important then, forty-five minutes ago, I meant that it, the party, was the beginning of the next stage, the next phase at Palmers Point, the reason for the turn it took, how it came to seem better for a time, at least in my opinion it was the reason.

But when I began thinking about that party in detail, when I came to think about what was actually *said* as against the impression he seemed to be making, which what was actually *said* I was going to skip over because time *is* running out—well then, when all this came back to me, God what a shock I did get. Because.

Well. The beginning, Pat, begin at the beginning and who knows, with writing it down you might even remember a few more important bits that have been sticking in the corners of your mind. Bits that you hadn't thought of as important up until now.

So. The party. The Raybourns' Thanksgiving Party which was really an Eve of Thanksgiving Party and their Wedding Anniversary Party, which was always something of an exclusive affair, just thirty or so guests and most of them Yacht Club people. The year before, we'd been invited but of course we were new then and the Raybourns' prodigies or whatever you call it, and of course Britishers, but this year as I say we were so far in the doghouse by this time that I felt like an old bone whenever Sylvia looked at me, and we, or at least I, got quite a shock to get the invite. *He* didn't seem surprised, just laughed and said, "Shall we turn them down, say we're having another baby?"—but as I said before he was ahead of me in knowing what I didn't. And he laughed even more when I took him seriously and said, "Good God, no, do you want us run out of Palmers Point altogether?" and he said, "Aha! I thought that *was* the point, the aim we've got in our sights." And I said, "Well not this way, not by being rude, yes, sure we'll go. But we'll wait until tomorrow before we tell them." "That's my girl," he said, and that was that, we accepted, and to tell the truth I was quite glad really, because it's all very well for Ron, he's out of it all day, five days a week. It's different when you're stuck in a place.

And then again, to tell the truth, I was curious about this new Ron of mine, and what was behind it, and I thought if it is some kind of promotion or something at work Charlie Raybourn will be sure to drop it out after he's had a few, and if it is a woman, and they've got an idea, Sylvia Raybourn or one of the other bitches will also be sure to let it slip.

Well, as I say, it was the usual sort of Raybourn party but even more exclusive and lavish. A million fancy dips and canapes of all kinds, most of them homemade, she goes to classes and you have to hand it to her, and the drink all first class and all out front, none of the usual sneaky Palmers Point business of having the best Scotch and the best gin back in the kitchen for the Inner Circle to sneak back to every so often, while the cheap stuff is dished out in the bar and sometimes, mark you (the things they'll stoop to), after being decanted into Johnnie Walker or Beefeater bottles, and as if it ever worked, because all that happens is after the first hour the kitchen trail gets caught on to and the men all crowd in there, Inner and Outer Circles both, and it gets like a poker school with the women left bitching out front. No, I'll say that for the Raybourns, they didn't go in for that sort of thing, not on these Thanksgiving do's, but then again of course it was *all* Inner Circle then, or nearly all, not counting us, and they couldn't very well work it on just two of us, could they?

Now, now, Pat, don't be like that. Give the Devil his, her, due. And it was well organized, not only with the food and the main liquor, but with the light stuff, even that—no crummy claret cup you never know what goes into it, but champagne for those who wanted it. Not well-known champagne, of course, more a sparkling white really, Ron told me, but at least it was French, not that domestic stuff which some might like but which tastes like nothing on earth, and it did taste like champagne and it was lovely.

So anyway, I've gone into all this because you'd have thought with the money and planning gone into it (they even had the foresight to get the Zetlinger girls, Mandy and Tricia, help serve, instead of any of the other teenagers, so there couldn't possibly be any unpleasantness with Harry and his Wandering Hands, not with his own daughters)—you'd have thought it would have gone with a swing right from the word go.

But no. When we arrived, even though we were a bit late and everybody else seemed to be there, you'd have thought it was a wake—except most wakes I've been to have been quite cheerful affairs even so early in the proceedings. Anyway, there they all were, with Charlie sweating already, obviously feeling the burden when he came laughing to let us in, with his great "Yee*ack!* Yee*ack!*" noise, false as false, false as the little squeeze he gives all his lady guests when he kisses them at the door. Yes. There they all were, just standing around in little groups and as soon as I saw them there I thought, "Hello, what's up?"

For one horrible minute, well, quarter-minute, I thought maybe it was us, maybe us being invited. Maybe we're still in the doghouse with them, no matter what the Raybourns have decided, oh my God. And I do believe I would have turned and run, or at least thrown a faint or something, if Ron hadn't been so cool and cheerful and just breezed in the way he did.

Anyway, it wasn't us. As I found out later it had been Mort Adams, who'd already had a few when we arrived, who'd blurted out, about five or ten minutes before, I can just see him:

"Hey! You'll just about be approaching the second Itch then, Charlie, huh? You'd best keep an eye on him, Sylv."

That was when he'd heard it was the Raybourns' *thirteenth* wedding anniversary, get it? Well of course you do, but I wouldn't have put it past Mort to have rubbed it in, not seeing the ice creeping down, by saying it himself:

"Get it? Two sevens're fourteen. *Seven-year* Itch."

Well all right, maybe with most couples it wouldn't have mattered. But how was he to know that Sylvia hadn't in fact had trouble with Charlie at the seven-year mark? Or Charlie with Sylvia, if it comes to that? Or if Sylvia was having one of her extra-suspicious bouts right now, over some new secretary of Charlie's? I mean with people as touchy as Sylvia . . .

Or maybe there was nothing at all, but everyone else thought there might be and started looking at Sylvia out of their eye corners and suddenly changing the subject, so that although it might have passed over her back it was impossible now, the way they'd all reacted. I mean maybe that had *triggered* a new bout. And maybe Charlie had reacted with one of those guilty signs only their wives know about.

Anyway, there it was. An Atmosphere. All ready for us to step into.

And guess what.

Who do you think cleared it up?

Who was it had them all forgetting it, even Sylvia, even poor Mort Adams, who wasn't knowing where to look by then, I bet?

Ronald Bracknell is who. My Ron. The last man I'd ever have expected to pull it off the way he did, or even try to.

But this was the New Ron. And this—now just listen to this and tell me if you don't think it is important—is how he did it.

"Well, well," said Harry Zetlinger, booming it out, not meaning it to be snide, just desperate to break that creeping ice cap, I can tell now, "the British have come. Hi, Pat, Ron."

"British?" Ron was grinning, looking around, over his shoulder, eyebrows up. "Who would that be?" he said. "Goddam British *here*, at a Thanksgiving Party?"

"Now what's that supposed to mean?" said Mort Adams, looking glad of the diversion, grinning himself, winking at everyone. "You trying to tell us you're taking out papers already or something?"

"Nah!" said Ron, sounding very American, more American than I'd ever heard him. Then he gave a little shudder, shook his head, blinked, and thanked Charlie for the vodka martini he'd had to mix special for Ron. "Sorry about that," he said, British again, "it's just"—he took a sip—"just that it was *him* again."

Something about all this had everybody staring, me included, smiling but a bit uneasy, but uneasy in a different way from the Atmosphere earlier.

"Him?"

"Yes. I—you see, folks," Ron looked around, pretending still to look worried, but laughing in his eyes, "I've had this strange experience."

"Oh, tell us, tell us!" squealed one of the women, Muriel I think.

"Yeah, tell us," everyone else seemed to start saying all at once.

"My body's been taken over," said Ron.

"Hurray, a ghost story!"

"By an American, I presume," said Harry Zetlinger, smooth now, seeing the way to a thaw, feeding Ron.

"Yes," said Ron, sighing. "An American, I'm afraid."

"Who doesn't like Scotch and water, obviously," said Harry.

Ron jumped. Honest, he was putting on a marvelous act. "How—how do *you* know?"

"Because you've switched to martinis," said Harry.

"Vodka martinis at that!" said Charlie, glad to get in on the act.

"Yes. Well," said Ron. "He—he does prefer it." Suddenly he grinned. "Hey, let's drink to him. Let's drink to the guy, the fanciest party-crasher in history—Otis P. Newstrander."

"Oh, *him!*" someone said, pretending to know the name.

Ron gave a sharp look, then grinned and said: "Yes. Otis P. Newstrander."

"Where's he from? Mars? Venus?"

"Nuh-huh," said Ron. "I told you. He's an American. Comes from, *came* from, Harrisburg, Pennsylvania."

"And he's dead, right?" someone said.

"His body is," said Ron. Then lifted his glass. "But Otis Newstrander—the *essential* Otis Newstrander—lives!"

"Otis Newstrander lives!" yelled some of the others, lifting their glasses.

"Viva Newstranda!" yelled Mort Adams, way behind.

"How come he took over *your* body?" said Harry, hunching his shoulders, making like a TV lawyer.

"I was asleep, Your Honor," said Ron. "I was just minding my own business, fast asleep."

"Can you vouch for this, ma'am?" said Harry, swinging toward me.

"I protest!" said Charlie Raybourn. "Being married to the accused, my client need not give evidence."

He put his hand on my shoulder and patted me, and I knew he was so glad then, so glad that Ron had started all this. Even Sylvia was smiling at me again, I mean genuine smiling.

"She wasn't there," said Ron.

"Aha!" said Harry.

"It was on my way back from—from upstate," said Ron, and I can remember now, as clear as if it was only yesterday, the way he

59

hesitated. "I was getting hypnotized by all this easy American driving, all your beautiful roads, and I decided to pull into a rest area and take a nap."

"Witnesses?"

"None, Your Honor. I just fell asleep and along came Otis, the Soul of Otis—"

"Hoo! Sounds like a Creature Feature!" squealed one of the girls.

"You also sneezed, right?"

"I guess I did. Yes. I sneezed as I snoozed—"

"And shezzam! In slipped Otis?"

"Right."

"Freshly dead, I presume?"

"Oh, sir, very. Very dead. Very fresh."

"By accident or foul means?"

"Well—"

"Answer my question!"

"Yeah! Answer! Answer!" we all yelled.

"Well the coroner said it was suicide."

"The hell with the coroner, what does Otis say?"

"Yeah. What does Otis say?"

"What does Otis's wife say?"

"Did he have a wife?"

"Did he have a *hat?*"

"Otis," said Ron, bowing his head and closing his eyes, "says he was murdered."

"*Did* he have a wife?"

"Otis's wife—whose name is Annette, incidentally—Mrs. Annette Newstrander also says it was murder."

"Maybe she did it."

"Not a chance. Annette was away visiting with friends in Baltimore when Otis got his."

"So she says!"

"So she *was*, the bitch!"

"Aha! Otis talking *now*."

"Yeah!" said Ron, in the snarly American voice again. "An' I could beat the hell out of her for it!"

"Oh, Pat! What's it like being married to *two* men?"

"Wonderful!" I said, pretending to lick my lips, little knowing of course.

"I'd settle for Ron," said Brenda Hunter, who was getting quite stewed.

"You would!" I thought.

"The other sounds like a typical American brute," said Brenda, looking at her husband.

"So what was Otis's job?" said Harry.

"That's just it," said Ron, British again. "His wife says they killed him because of it."

"Who's they?"

"Mafia."

"How? Shooting?"

"Poison."

"Those dirty wops!" Gene Piscola grinned.

"*What* job? Numbers runner?"

"Insurance assessor."

"Aha!" said Harry. "He'd stumbled on to something, right?"

"Tell me," said Mort Adams, leering at me, not Ron, "he have any more conflicting habits, this Otis, besides liking vodka 'stead of Scotch?"

"Yes!" I giggled, being on my third drink by now. "He prefers jockey shorts to the other kind."

That got a laugh. Even Ron joined in and I was glad because if there had been a woman caused him to change he would have been pulled up sharp. But he wasn't and I was so happy and now everybody else was and it started a kind of game, a kind of fancy dress without the dress if you get me, with everyone pretending their bodies had been taken over too, guess by who, and it really seemed to catch fire, and when the party was over later that night Sylvia came with us all down the driveway saying "Thank you! Thank you! Thank you!" and I'm pretty sure it wasn't only because we'd helped put Charlie to bed.

Anyway.

Anyway, it was after that we got this new lease on life in Palmers Point, socially I mean, with everyone inviting us again, and so naturally it was important.

But now I've remembered the actual *words*. Now that I can see it wasn't just any bit of kidding—now that I've seen what was *behind* it—

Well.

Ron doesn't mention it in his diary. Not about what he actually said. And of course he has his own ideas about the change after Cleveland.

All the same.

I don't know.

Oh, snap out of it, Pat. Look at the time, three already, let's go over what he *did* write about that time, then perhaps we'll *see*.

His Journal:
Entry Number 3

There has now been a sufficient lapse of time for me to be able to assess some of the more enduring effects of Experiment One (I use that designation advisedly, I'm afraid, as will be apparent), together with reservations, the more recent of which have proved to be so unexpectedly considerable.

The most immediate effect, as I had predicted, was in the realm of self-confidence. (I am speaking now of the more settled period, after the first euphoria had faded—the mere, somewhat unworthy elation at "having got away with it.") This boost to the self-confidence was, however, of a vastly different quality, a different *feel*, to anything I had anticipated. By this I mean that there was in it something almost chemical. There was no intermittency, no forgetting of the experiment only to be pulled up, braced, by the memory. No lapsing into old negative attitudes. No fading of effect.

It was instead as if something had been released into my bloodstream, some glandular secretion of which I had experienced a deficiency all my life. This is not to say that I had been acutely conscious of any abiding abnormality before. I had suspected something of the kind, certainly, but then there were so many others who seemed to be in the same case that it could hardly be considered as abnormal, could it? Nevertheless, with the increase in supply of this substance, this chemical, this secretion—with the clearing of its channels, as it were—I realized for the first time what true normalcy means.

There is a sense of equilibrium so strong that it would seem—actually did seem, for weeks—impossible that one should ever be caught off balance again, psychologically as well as physically.

There is a sense of calm—no doubt engendered by that enhancement of equilibrium.

There is a vastly increased stock of energy—or, probably more accurately, a vastly increased resistance to fatigue. Again this seems natural enough, given the new calm, the new balance, ensuring the easing of tensions and the elimination of false alarms that one's nervous system "normally" is subjected to.

But as I say, the usual is not really normal. This is the *true* condition of normalcy. This is what feels so *right*.

To put it another way, it is the difference between wearing ill-fitting shoes and those that have been hand-made, not only according to the physical measurements of one's feet, but also with regard to one's walking habits and peculiarities of gait, etc. A man can go through life in the former type of shoes, attributing the various foot discomforts encountered—soreness, corns, hammer toes, swollen ankles, or whatever—to "normal" wear and tear, when all the time this might have been obviated, given the necessary knowledge (and of course means).

Such then was the basic effect. Chemical. I am convinced.

This is not to say that one's mental processes played no part in it. They did—if only in a supporting role. Thus whenever anyone annoyed me—someone at work, say, or some negligent or insolent clerk in a store—I was able to keep cool, quite cold, quite undisturbed, thinking:

"I am capable of killing you. Not you *exactly*, maybe, but someone just like you."

I was able to think this not only quite coolly, but also happily, contentedly—knowing that what I was thinking was absolutely true —and this showed, it came with the smile, it went with the eyes. Time and time again I noticed its effect: the quick back-off, the sudden slight double-take, the taking *thought*—and by that I mean the other person *thinking* for a change. Just as if he or she had actually heard the words that had come to my mind.

Yes, indeed. Yes, sir. They took notice all right. They still do.

And then, after I'd experienced this silent process a number of times, I—or the critic I set up inside myself, the observer, the scientific observer, because I my true self never had any doubts at all, because it was so right, the feeling was so consistent, so right, so true, so deep, so right—I decided to try it out loud, to test it that way.

And on such occasions, with a broader smile on my face, occasionally with a wink, but with steady eyes and a dead-calm voice, I would say:

"You know, someone might kill you one day for saying something like that."

And again, though it seemed on the surface like a joke, a bit grim perhaps but still a joke, it had its effect. Because it was said with knowledge and experience, and one's chemistry had its effect on the other person's chemistry. Snap. Like that. And the outer reaction was commensurately more immediate and definite.

I remember using those very words, the first time I applied the test in this way. I said it to a cab driver, after he'd started raging about the Mayor, about how "the guy ought to be run over by a truck one of these days when he's riding that goddam bicycle of his." I remember feeling mildly annoyed as "usual" by this arrogance, this presumption, this taking advantage of a captive audience. How the hell did he know that I wasn't an avid supporter of the Mayor? Even a relative? And if he didn't know, it meant he didn't care, so who the hell did he think I was, to sit there meekly taking it? Who was paying who, for Christ's sake?

That was the "normal" silent reaction, anyway. And I had experienced it enough times to know it could leave one feeling ruffled for hours. This time, however, although the same questions arose, they did so in a much cooler, more stable solution.

I leaned forward. I put my face very close to the back of his head so that I could see us both in the mirror, my eyes on his. Then I said softly, smiling:

"You know, someone might kill you one day for saying something like that."

His mouth opened, then closed. He didn't even demand to know if I was threatening him, because of course I wasn't.

But the message was received. The test was successful. The litmus had changed color. He was silent for the rest of the journey.

Did I mention that Raybourn was with me on that occasion?

Well, he was.

It was quite safe because, again, obviously, I didn't intend to kill the cabbie personally, or even *a* cabbie, if it came to that, so there was no question of creating a clue or establishing a motive. Yet once more the chemistry did its work. The fact that my remark was so un-expected and so heartfelt, yet delivered so quietly, had its effect on Raybourn too, the mere onlooker. He was struck, I could tell. Struck dumb. But I helped him out, turning to him as if nothing had happened and making pleasant commonplace conversation about the new decor in the reception area at the office.

This was just before Thanksgiving, just after I'd received confirmation of the success of Experiment One, in fact, and at first I thought the incident was the reason for his change of attitude, his new respect, resulting in an unexpected invitation to their Eve of Thanksgiving Party.

Indeed, I still think it had something to do with it, though I have to admit the probability that he'd already had wind of that first promotion of mine, which was to come through a few weeks later and so, by Christmas, place me parallel to him in the hierarchy and even give me just that *leetle* bit of edge in long-term prospects. Be that as it may, however, it still amounts to the same thing, for I shall always put down the promotion itself (a very close thing, by all accounts) to the new mana I was giving off, which had quite clearly been noticed by more than Raybourn, and more important people than he.

But to the matter in hand.

Why a second experiment?

Had I not achieved my object?

Wasn't that first one enough?

In fact, had I not conjectured so earlier, placing it on record in my early fumbling analogies to the Mafia situation—that one such killing was usually enough?

Because this, remember, was a sane scientific investigation. It was purely a question of cause and effect. It had nothing to do with madness, with strange unaccountable homicidal urges or anything of that kind.

So why?

An interesting question, or group of questions.

I think perhaps the chief factor in my decision to set up a second experiment has been Challenge. Challenge—that eminently scientific prime mover—supercharged by the regrettably emotional and therefore inflammatory agency of annoyance. Intense, totally unpredictable annoyance. Or, rather, to place it squarely and properly

66

in the post-Experiment-One context, annoyance of a totally unpredictable intensity that took me quite by surprise, even to the extent of radically disturbing the new-found balance.

Looking back with some measure of that balance restored—not all, alas, not by any means all—I fancy I can detect a certain irony in the circumstances, because the intensity of annoyance would probably have been nothing nearly so great in someone who had never killed, never carried through to a successful conclusion such an experiment as mine. But since one *had* been so successful, the whole situation became translated into terms of Power. In short, it was my power base that had been challenged and, it seemed, however irrationally, found wanting.

To put it another way and so at least perhaps clear up the irrational element:

If one has it in one's power to do something and neglects to do it, in circumstances that simply cry out for such an exercise, the psychic discomfort is acute.

Consider, for example, an expert card player who, for some reason, for any reason, misses an easy trick. Or a star soccer player who fails to score with the ball at his feet five yards away from an open goalmouth. Such a failure can put either off his game for hours, and even (by a cumulative process) months.

Now, although we can eliminate the irrational element by pointing out that it was not within my power to kill the mugger who had accosted me in the incident in question (I was unprepared, I had no suitable weapon), there was, theoretically, nothing to prevent me from taking up the challenge along the lines laid down in Bracknell's Law and killing some other mugger under suitably controlled conditions.

And that is what has been getting under my skin, further upsetting the balance, undermining my whole position.

But first let me describe the incident.

I had an early dinner engagement with an out-of-town client and he failed to turn up. This was not really surprising. It was January and one of those sudden short but heavy snowstorms had occurred in the early evening, just when he should have been setting off to join me. Since the restaurant I had chosen was one of those French places over on Ninth Avenue, and his hotel was right over on the East Side, near the U.N. building, I could sympathize with his suggestion to postpone the meeting when he called the restaurant and told me of the impossibility of getting a cab from where he was. I myself had been very lucky in that respect, and had not had so far to travel from the office.

Being there already, however, I decided to have the meal alone and hope that the storm would subside while I was eating, and in fact this is what happened. When I emerged, the sky was clear. But the streets were not, of course, and although the covering was not as deep as I'd feared and a certain amount of traffic was on the move, the cab drivers were still apparently back in their hideouts, blaming it all on the Mayor, no doubt.

So, not really too put out, I started the trek to Grand Central, glad at least that I'd had the foresight to come equipped with rubber overshoes.

It was while cutting through one of the Forties between Eighth and Broadway that the incident occurred.

Maybe I should have stuck to one of the major crosstown streets. But there is something about a fresh blanket of snow that displaces one's normal lines of judgment. Or at least there was something about *that* fresh blanket that displaced *mine*. For, apart from the general dislocation that caused me to be walking anyway, and seeking to go by the most direct route, there was the false sense of natural cleanliness, of renewal, of—well—something magical. It was not that one felt there had been a temporary suspension in *all* the usual after-dark activities of the city, that the muggers too were remaining under cover, along with the cab drivers, banished by this soft white magic and waiting for it to blacken and turn to slush. No. One just didn't think about them at all. One forgot them completely. Anyway, I did, until—when I was passing by a new building excavation, unwisely close to the hoarding—he emerged.

He was quite short, in a thick plaid knee-length coat, hunched inside it, dejectedly I thought at first, black, with hair that was either graying or sprinkled with snow, I couldn't quite tell. I never did get the chance to ascertain which, either, because when we came together and he said, "Hey, excuse me, mister," in a voice as warm and smooth as drinking chocolate, my eyes became fixed on the blade.

He held it casually, like something he'd just picked up from the ground, as if he was about to ask whether I'd dropped it myself.

"Just stay nice and loose, huh? Just stay right there and slo-o-owly, nice and easy, hand me that bag."

All at once I felt very scared. Oddly enough, it wasn't so much fear of being stabbed to death there and then as simply being cut by the thing, and badly infected.

But scared. Trembling. Shaken to my foundations.

That was the main thing.

No question of drawing on my new-found confidence, strength, balance.

No confidence. No strength. No balance.

All I wanted was to get away uncut.

I slowly lifted my briefcase, desperately anxious not to have any movement misinterpreted. I was sweating.

Then suddenly the blade disappeared. He turned. I still held the bag in what must have seemed like a posture of dismayed rejection, as he hurried away.

Then the headlamps arched fully into the street and cast my shadow along the snow and the car came alongside.

"You O.K. there?"

The policemen were looking up at me curiously.

"I—er—"

They still stared, taking me in, head to toes, taking inventories, making checks. Quite obviously, my man had seen them before they had seen him, while they were turning. It was me and me alone they were interested in.

"I was just wondering if I was going in the right direction for Grand Central Station," I said.

They relaxed. The British accent, which I'd laid on thick, did its usual disarming work.

"Long ways from Charing Cross, huh?" said the nearer one, grinning, pronouncing it "Chairing."

I laughed.

"I was beginning to think I might get *there* sooner than Grand Central," I said. "*Is* this the way?"

And so, in banter, the incident was closed.

In banter outwardly; in furious seething anger within.

Because I had been challenged and had lost something much more precious than briefcase or wallet or watch.

Tell those cops? I would as soon have complained to the British Embassy or written to the *Palmers Point News* to ask for Abby's advice.

No. I wanted that fucker for myself.

The unparliamentary term must be excused. Because that is how

I framed it in my mind as I forced a grin for those cops, a mild one, bland old British lopsided grin, what.

"I want that fucker for myself!"

And I actually wept hot tears of baffled fury as I went on my way, knowing that this would hardly be possible, that only a miracle could ever bring me face to face with him again, in suitable circumstances.

That fury had spent itself by the time I reached the station. But the incident continued to rankle.

For I *had* been caught off balance. The chemistry had been seriously upset. New secretions had jetted into my system—secretions released by acute fear and acute frustration and cataclysmic fury—and although their effect gradually abated, they are still here.

Oh yes, they are still here.

And the result has been deplorable.

When I got home I snapped at Pat as I had never done in months.

At work I lost my temper more than once, several times, shocking some, giving immense satisfaction to others.

And the worst of it is that one thing leads to another, with a chain reaction getting established, and ground—much magnificent, hard-won, dearly bought ground—being lost as a consequence.

Why, only the other day I snapped at Pat again, in public too, at the first big party we ourselves had thrown, her birthday, and all because of that two-bit little creep bastard with the knife and the unforeseen difficulties in implementing the Law in this particular case.

Well, it cannot be allowed to continue.

One has no choice but to draw up detailed plans for Experiment Two and proceed to rectify the balance, no matter how great the difficulties.

I shall give it my closest attention from now on.

70

Her Journal:
Entry Number 8

Well of course that's been one good thing, anyway. I mean about snapping at me those times. Knowing it was nothing to do with me really, I mean. That's one good thing to come out of it, Pat.

Because believe me I got quite a shock. Snapping at me is something he doesn't do much of at any time in any circumstances, and especially not in company the way some men do, I don't know how their wives stand it, I really don't, and over here where I expected women would never stand for it at all you'd be surprised how often it happens. Brenda Hunter is always getting it and sometimes she looks quite sick but she never snaps back, and even Muriel Adams has to put up with it, when Mort comes over all bitter and sarcastic after the seventh or eighth drink, but then they say that's the only time he does do it and she makes him pay at all others. Even Charlie Raybourn can snap very quietly sometimes, like I suppose a turtle snaps with the same kind of slit mouth and all Sylvia does is go on smiling, smiling, as if she'd never heard.

But maybe it's just in Palmers Point it happens so often.

Anyway, Ronald never makes a habit of it with me, I will say that, he never has, even in bad nervy times. Grumpy, yes, he gets then. And quiet, very quiet, doesn't seem to hear. We had lots of that that first year in P.R.P., I can tell you, and very exasperating it is too, but snapping—very rarely.

When it happens, maybe because it is so rare, I go all of a jelly, all to pieces, honest, I can't help it, I'm not trying to pay him out or anything but that's the way it takes me. Everything from under my feet. End of the world. Oh, horrible, really. And why I say I'm not trying to pay him out is because when I do crumple like that it really crucifies him, hurts him much worse than it hurts me, has *him* crumpling in a way, and I hate to see it but I can't help it, talk about tearing each other to shreds. And although it's lovely to make it up afterward and hear him saying how there's nothing, nothing in the world Pat cuts me up worse than seeing you hurt and knowing I'm responsible, it's not so lovely that it's worth going through the agony for, believe me.

So, that night in January.

"The snow, the bloody snow, woman, what d'you *think* delayed me?"

Well, I was only asking. I wasn't even complaining.

And what made it so much worse was the fact that this came after a long shining happy period that started round about Thanksgiving and went on through the promotion and the holidays and seemed all set to last forever.

I started wondering again if there wasn't a woman. *Had* it been a business client stood him up in that restaurant that night? I mean Ron's never been the type to get mad at what *clients* do. All part of the game, he says, said it many a time. Business colleagues some-times, yes. They'll get him mad. But never clients. And never just a bit of rough weather and having to wait around in the cold or wet. So I mean it was only natural I should think it was a woman, and even though I dropped that idea after a bit, it was always a puzzle, and now it's quite a relief in a way to know what really happened. Poor lamb.

I suppose the reason I dropped the woman idea was because this mood—just grumpy, just quiet most of the time, not snappy, not till my party that night anyway—was because it lasted, day after day, week after week, and with women when they're the cause, when they're pulling the strings, it's more up-and-downy, either that or it blows over and men soon forget them. So then I got to wondering if it wasn't business colleagues after all, something at work, and I sup-pose that's what made me more anxious than ever about this party, about it being a big hit, and why I was so jumpy and nervy, and why it seemed to be catching, right from the minute the very first people arrived, so that it didn't matter if we had spent a fortune on the best booze, Beefeater and Johnnie Walker for everyone, and even Wild

Turkey for the bourbon drinkers and real Moet and Chandon for the light brigade, even if it was non-vintage. The whole thing started freezing up from the word go, and I panicked and I suppose I did have too much of the champagne too quickly and I started talking sixty to the dozen and saying all sorts of things, right up until the moment when Ron saw his chance, when I was going for more ice and he snapped—in a whisper, I'll admit, but so fierce it seemed worse than if he'd yelled at me:

"For Christ's sake, pull yourself together!"

Well, that was it. I just collapsed. Everyone thought I'd passed out with the champagne, pooped out at my own party, and maybe it was just as well. Ron told me afterward, next morning, full of remorse, haggard he was, that everyone was very sympathetic, and Charlie Raybourn was lovely, making them all laugh, saying, "What the hell, Ron. It's her party. Let the kid pass out if she wants. I'm doing it all the time. Relax, man. Five'll get you ten that there'll be at least three others pass out, we're not used to such good liquor at most of the parties around here." And in fact three more did pass out that night, at *least* three more, and what Charlie said did somehow break the ice, and I've always had a soft spot for him every since, even though I suppose he was being a bit snide at someone or other saying that, maybe the New Year's wassail-bowl fiasco at the Leemans'.

Anyway, it's nice to know what really was at the back of the snapping. Even in all this troubling business there's a bit of good news if you look for it.

But "troubling" is the word.

Just look at this next bit.

His Journal:
Entry Number 4

PROBLEMS INVOLVED IN IMPLEMENTING
ONE'S DECISION TO KILL A MUGGER

This is not easily effected, when the random nature of the operation is a prime consideration.

To kill a certain definite mugger—say the man who accosted me, assuming that I know his identity and address, etc.—is something else entirely. It has its own attendant risks, of course, in that my knowledge of this information would presuppose certain links, along one of which it may be possible eventually to trace the responsibility for his death to me. But that constitutes a post-operational problem. The preliminaries—of seeking out, of reconnaissance, of picking a suitable time to strike—present no obstacles of any appreciable size.

But in conformity with Bracknell's Law, the whole matter is stood on its head. Post-operational problems scarcely exist when no direct pre-determined links exist; whereas the preliminaries pose questions of immense difficulty, if not complexity.

Because first, to paraphrase Mrs. Beeton, one must catch one's mugger. And, immediately, the question of identification arises. Mrs. Beeton's hare (I think it was a hare, let us assume it was) had long ears, a certain coloring, a certain way of moving, a certain habitat, and—in the one respect in which confusion might arise—certain distinctive features to mark it out from its near relative, the rabbit. Only a fool could make a mistake, even in this last respect, when

74

telling details could be checked beforehand, without the need for forging any particular and therefore incriminating link, viz., by looking up those differences in some good reference book.

But with muggers it is quite another matter. We may suspect a certain lurker or group of lurkers to be muggers, from their general behavior, the way they move or don't move, even to some extent from their dress. Yet how can we be sure that these are not ordinary layabouts, panhandlers perhaps, but rabbits, not hares?

It must be very easy for *some* huntsmen. I refer of course to the bigoted or crazy, rather than to the legitimate licensed wartime killer, whose lack of problems in this respect needs hardly be stressed. After all, it was for his convenience that uniforms were invented. A glimpse of field gray or khaki—and bang! bang! Nothing to it, so long as it was you who caught the first glimpse of the other. No. But even the bigoted or crazy have few problems, the first because of the very color of the quarry's skin, or the shape of his skull, or his name, or the quasi-uniform to which a gamekeeping bigots' government has thoughtfully confined him, say a Star of David emblazoned back and front (and constituting an ideal target); and the second, the crazy, because all that matters to them is that the quarry should possess a certain arbitrary distinction, like red hair, or be a woman of a certain age (we have touched on this above), or a person following a certain easily identifiable profession.

How then *is* one, with any acceptable degree of sureness, to identify a mugger?

The answer is, unfortunately:

In only two ways.

These are:

(a) by proven and known repute; and

(b) by apprehending him in the very act of mugging.

Now, it has already been suggested that inquiries essential to the pursuit of course (a) are too likely to draw attention to the hunter. Even if in the first instance such inquiries are pursued by remote control, by studying the newspapers, by noting the names and addresses of convicted muggers, say, there must come the moment of the direct question:

"Is that where Leroy Howard lives?"

Or:

"Has he been released yet?"

Or:

"Is *that* Leroy Howard, the short one, the stocky one, the one in the plaid coat?"

And even if one evades such a bald approach, and hangs around, asking nothing, merely listening for the casual identifying greeting, say ("Hi, Leroy, they let you out already?"), well, that takes time and time creates over-exposure. ("Why, yes, officer, there has been a stranger hanging around here lately. Figured he was one of you fellers, matter of fact. Tall guy, black hair, he followed Leroy in here, asked for cigarettes with a British accent. . . .")

No good.

The more one considers it, the more one is forced to the conclusion that the quarry will have to be run to earth by method (b)— and that has its own serious difficulties.

Thus:

Although it makes for certain identification, it quite considerably shortens the chances of success. For consider. Supposing one to be successful in acting as one's own decoy, what happens if there are too many of the bastards at the moment of contact? The huntsman's great advantage in this game is that of surprise, but this is only truly effective if the quarry operates alone, or at the very most in pairs. With a gun or even with a knife, given a sufficient element of surprise, the single mugger may be taken care of. With two of them, the knife is ruled out (one is also assuming here a degree of proficiency, and that is not easily acquired) and the gun must be resorted to. Even then it may not be as effective as a shotgun of some kind, but that poses its own problems of adequate concealment and ready application. Granted that in the case of a group confrontation one might always be reasonably sure of taking one of them out before being killed oneself, but what good is that? This is no suicide operation, no half-crazy desire for revenge. If it were, a simple grenade ("Sure, fellers, take my wallet, take my watch, here and take this too") would suffice.

One might of course embark on a calculated risk, being ready to use a gun or a knife in the case of a single assailant, and equally ready to hand it over, together with the wallet, watch, etc., in the case of two or more. But then one would be at their mercy, and not all of the bastards are prepared to leave it at loot. What irony to have one's throat slit before being able to complete the operation. What price Bracknell's Law then?

76

That is an aspect that will demand *very* careful attention. For it automatically rules out what might have been an excellent alternative weapon: poison again. Little as the prospect of repeating oneself appeals, this did seem to have its points on first reflection. The pack of candies laced with cyanide; the bottle of Scotch again. It would work, certainly. What mugger would suspect such a trick? Yet if the huntsman's throat were slit before his weapon had struck home, what joy would there be in that?

At least then we have narrowed down the question of *means* (leaving aside for the time being the knottier problem of how to be a decoy without letting it reduce one's chances too severely). The logical choice would seem to fall between gun or knife.

Which?

The knife has its obvious appeal, just as it does for the muggers themselves. It is easily concealed; it may be fairly easily explained away should it be accidentally discovered; and above all it is silent. Yes, it certainly has its points (as well as its point, if one may be permitted a jest, as one should, for it relaxes, and whatever relaxes in such operations has its value). And yet, and yet. One can't help feeling that a greater degree of expertise would be necessary than one is capable of mustering.

Let us imagine that scene back in January.

The hoarding. The emergent shadow.

"Hey, excuse me, mister!"

And the knife. His knife.

It is there already. Long, sharp, and about two inches from one's navel. Casually held, granted, but probably only seemingly so, and certainly *expertly* held.

Well?

One dithers. One disarms the other in *that* respect.

One pretends to tremble, one even begins to plead, ready to draw and slash—one movement, from inside pocket high on left, backhanded across his throat.

Sounds simple. But:

"Just stay nice and loose, huh? Just stay right there and slo-o-owly—"

Remember?

The caution?

One may not have pleaded then, but one had trembled all right. Oh yes, one was obviously an easy mark all right. But, nevertheless, he had remained very cautious. And if one had had a knife in the inside pocket high on the left, it would probably have got no further than to glint in the open before—*shuck!*—his was in your gut, deep.

(The projection is of more than eliminative value. It has just occurred to me that if, or rather when, such an operation is mounted, it will be with some kind of leather or even steel protector for the abdomen. Whatever one's own weapon should be.)

No. Even equipped with such protection, the knife seems to be ruled out. For note this: *that one backhanded slash would have to do it.* One is out to kill and kill immediately, not maim, and that requires an expert.

A gun then? It is beginning to look like it. One advantage that springs to mind is the fact that I have at least some little experience in the field, left over from National Service days. Another, arising naturally from the essence of Bracknell's Law, is that there should be no dangers in using one per se: the crime-book rigmarole of checking with ballistics to prove that this gun killed that person only really figures when the motive involves closer, traceable, personal links. And God knows there should be no difficulty in acquiring one with a sufficient measure of anonymity in *this* country. And then again, even if it should be discovered before one has had time to make the kill (it won't matter afterward, because then it will have outlived its usefulness and will be ditched there and then, simply tossed onto the body), well, in such an event it will scarcely seem remarkable. Most of the people here have guns in their houses against the black revolution they're always dithering about. And if one does a great deal of traveling, alone . . .

No, the real problem about guns is that they are so bloody noisy. Here indeed does a Bracknell killing present a post-operational problem, let us say an *immediate*-p.o. problem, and a very tricky one.

Because noise attracts witnesses and witnesses might hamper one's getaway.

Are there such things as silencers, I wonder?

And, if so, are they so clumsy as to make concealment difficult, or accuracy debatable?

Questions, questions.

But they will have to be sifted, tested, explored. That much is very clear.

His Journal:
Entry Number 5

Strange how the act of preparation can soothe, when one is sure of one's ultimate capability to do the deed one prepares for.

A month has elapsed now since that encounter after the snow-storm, and I feel an almost perfect equanimity even though I still haven't decided on the time, or place, or type of gun.

But yes: it shall be a gun. On that I have decided. And this in turn brings me closer to a choice of location, because the logistics in such a case demand that I think in terms of almost certainly attracting attention, witnesses, and how to avoid recognition (to say nothing of apprehension) by them.

Had I decided on a knife, for example, this question of possible witnesses would not be so obtrusive. The silence of such a weapon, as I indicated above, would be—is—a decided advantage, and advantages must be maximized. Therefore one would have been logically directed to the choice of a comparatively quiet, little-frequented place that is nevertheless a likely spot for muggers. Certain stretches of Central Park spring readily to mind, only to be almost equally readily rejected. For by all accounts this place (one is thinking now of the night, of course) is unfrequented only by the innocent. In short, one is confronted by a possibility that comes close to being a probability: that one sticks one's knife into a mugger, leaving it in or by the body as prudence dictates, only to be mugged while making one's getaway. Amusing, perhaps; somewhat exaggerated, perhaps; but with too much truth in it not to constitute a severe warning.

Still thinking in terms of a knife, then, one directs one's attention to a different locale: a place presenting all the requisite desiderata without the drawback outlined. And before long there comes to mind what would seem to be, still seems to be, the ideal spot. I refer to a certain section of New York south of Greenwich Village (or in the southern part of the Village itself, I am not exactly sure)—anyway, a place of warehouses and quiet streets, yet with the attraction of a popular night club, a jazz place, one that Pat and I were taken to during our first stay in the city. Between it and the more populated areas of the Village there must be a number of lurkers at any given time of the night, as I remember our host remarking at the time, insisting that we take a cab and no chances. Yet because the club is one of the very few places to attract people away from the mainstream, that number of muggers should be proportionately small, so that the Central Park situation would be unlikely to arise.

However, such a problem only obtains in the case of a knife and, as indicated already, I had soon rejected that weapon on technical grounds, just as I have also rejected the idea of using a silencer, after making a few discreet inquiries and giving it careful consideration in their light. (The home manufacture of such an article requires an expertise I do not possess, while its purchase ready-made immediately advertises the fact that the weapon is for offensive rather than defensive use. Further, even if one were to come into possession of a silencer without arousing unwelcome suspicion, its assembly prior to use could render the augmented weapon less easy to conceal, as I had prefigured, while its assembly at the point of operation would consume vital seconds. And anyway, according to some accounts, silencers do indeed—also as I had conjectured—diminish accuracy and efficiency to a far greater degree than the television scriptwriters would have us believe.) And when one then moves on to consider an unmuffled gun, the kind of place posited above is very quickly pushed out of the reckoning.

Consider. Little frequented though those streets may be at night, a gunshot report is sure to attract witnesses. Passing cabs. Worse—passing patrol cars. Night watchmen. Caretakers. People in upper windows. And in a near-deserted street, one hurrying figure is quickly spotted.

No. With guns one requires crowds, confusion, and the cover they provide, which must be the best there is. The street, the alley, the dark corner: that particular section of the locality will still have to be quiet enough, of course, if only to make it a likely place for the initiating hold-up. But the crowds must be just around that corner—ready and emboldened by mere numbers to come flocking, craning their silly necks, offering their beautiful cover. People who need people include more than sentimental torch singers. Assassins too need people, it seems, and just as desperately, in certain circumstances.

Even as I write this I am mentally humming that song. For of course it is perfect, it is poetic, it is so fitting, that such eminently practical considerations should finally point to the very location in which it all started: out there in the West Forties, between Broadway and Eighth, or Eighth and Ninth. *That* is where it shall be completed then, once I have decided on the type of gun. And who knows: fate, this beautifully logical process, may serve up to me again that little bastard in the plaid coat.

Meanwhile, I have been content enough to devise the protector I wrote about in the last entry.

That was an excellent idea, but not as easy to translate into practical terms as might have seemed at first. Glancing back, I see that it was originally conceived as "some kind of leather or even steel protection for the abdomen."

Well—what?

In effect I had given (granting that the protection to be afforded was against blades rather than bullets) an almost verbatim dictionary definition of an orthodox shield, and that of course was out of the question. One cannot walk along busy streets with a shield on one's arm without attracting attention, even in Manhattan, and anyway, all a skillful assailant has to do is change his angle of approach. Too absurd even to have been mentioned? Perhaps. But one becomes increasingly convinced that the propounding of absurdities in the early stages of problem-solving yields great riches in a practical vein when taken a stage or two further. For the notion of visibility, the undesirability of visibility in a shield, at once drew me on to consider *in*visibility in a shield; in other words, perfect concealment.

Warmer.

Abdomen, shield, leather, steel . . . Stop. Eliminate the last term and what do we have? One of those leather devices that boxers wear under their trunks.

Excellent.

But: here one must refer back to the nature of Bracknell's Law, its terms, the stress it lays on the maximization of such natural advantages as casualness, anonymity, the camouflage of normalcy. Unless one is a boxer, the possession of such an article (too bulky to be easily concealed when not in use) is bound to arouse curiosity, create suspicion. Even more than if one should be discovered to possess a gun, in these times, in this place.

So: could some suitable substitute be devised that would eliminate this objection? Some article or group of articles of everyday significance—or, more correctly, insignificance.

At first I toyed with the idea of improvising with a strip of carpeting from the car, simply lifting it out when required and retiring somewhere to wind it, doubled, around my waist, under my shirt.

Not very good.

The dimensions were such that, doubled, it became too bulky for comfort and too difficult to keep in place even with a belt. And even then it was doubtful if it would withstand a really determined thrust from a sharp knife.

But the idea of something that could be carried around in the car, with a perfect excuse for being there—this appealed—and before long I remembered the fishing stool.

Something of a white elephant, because I don't fish, it had appealed to me when I bought it, in a souvenir store at the airport in Dallas, as being a useful picnic stool: *something to carry around in the trunk of the car, in fact—where indeed it had remained all through winter.*

And why did this recommend itself instantly, as soon as it came to mind? Because it consists of three wooden legs, centrally pivoted and thereby collapsible, and a large triangle of the stoutest leather imaginable, saddle-stitched and tooled with a cow's-head design. At each of the three corners is a pouch, into which the upper end of each leg is fitted when the stool is assembled—though that is by the way in this context.

But there it was. The hunk of leather, as perfectly shaped for the protection of one's abdomen as for the seat of a stool. I tried it out in the garage. Tailor-made.

At first it seemed as if it would be self-supporting—that merely slipping it into place down one's pants and under one's shirt would be sufficient. Indeed I was so convinced of this, so confident, that I left it where it was and went about my normal course in the house for an hour or so, quite certain that no one, not even Pat, would notice it. And I was right. With a jacket on, it was completely undetectable apart from a slight creak. I even left it on to drive round to the liquor store in, even forgot I had it on from time to time.

Yet there was a drawback. It had a tendency to slide around a little, and slip a little, so that the central of the three corners, worn downward, tended to jut at the crotch, giving one the appearance of a bullfighter accentuating his manhood. More to the point (or away from the point!), this tended to leave a strip of the soft upper abdomen exposed.

Some light but broad and tight underbelt seemed to be required to remedy this, something firm enough to hold the protector in place. I wondered about the possibility of using elasticized swimming trunks, and it was while I was rummaging around in the drawers in the third bedroom, looking for a pair, that I found the perfect answer: an old girdle of Pat's, one of the sort that went out of fashion with the coming of panty-hose and the semi-pants-type girdle to match.

It was white, quite plain, and without the suspender straps, which were easily removed, could quite well have passed for a man's body belt. A small man's, granted, but I pride myself on being quite slim in that part of the anatomy anyway, though perhaps it is as well that the garment had lost *some* at least of its elasticity.

Anyway, it was perfect. When not in use it could be rolled up, can be rolled up, is now rolled up, in a very small space, and locked away in the toolbox. And when *in* use, it holds the leather in place for hours, with absolutely no shifting or sliding.

I know this because I have tried it out, several times. On one of these occasions I actually wore it in situ, as it were, in the city itself one evening, on a dinner engagement with a client. I was quite surprised—even though I had anticipated something of the sort—to note the immense feeling of invulnerability it instigated.

This could be dangerous, I know.

But one keeps one's sense of proportion.

Her Journal:
Entry Number 9

Well all I can say is it isn't there now.

As soon as I read that bit about the girdle I went down into the basement to have a look in the toolbox but it wasn't there. I thought maybe I might have missed it being more taken with the book, but no. I pulled out the drawers and looked behind them to see if it had been rolled up tight and stashed away there, but no, no girdle.

And judging from what he's written about what happened since, it doesn't seem likely that he's still using it, got it with him now I mean, this trip. Though of course you never know. I mean if there is some truth in all this, if he really had been nearly mugged that time and he was scared enough to need to have some sort of protection, but there you are. One thing leads to another. What's he want to keep going where he's likely to get mugged *for?* Oh, I don't know. Don't ask me. I'm only his wife. But press on, Pat. Press on regardless and get it all down, every word, and then sleep on it, keep puzzling it all out, it'll come, you'll see, and if it doesn't then you can always try an expert, yes, he'll be able to tell.

Meantime, about this girdle business, I have to smile, and one thing reading about it, his version, has done is explain another little mystery.

Because I did miss it, you know. I didn't think so much about it at the time because believe me what was weighing on my mind more was this quietness of his, this sudden calm after the storm, after the snapping period, and I thought what now? What's brewing now? Anything, or should I just breathe easier and count my blessings? But even with all that going on in my head I did miss that girdle and I even connected it with him but only for a very short time, just joking really, and then I forgot about it, so I can't claim to be very clever really. No.

But looking back, I could kick myself because if I had given it more thought I might have been able to get to the bottom of all this right then, maybe even challenged him, so that the joking part might have come in useful, shaking him and shaming him into telling the truth, mentioning this thing about muggers that was building up, and then one thing leading to another so that it all came out, all this Bracknell's Law stuff, these daydreams, the Cleveland trip, all of it. They say it's so much easier to clear things like that up if you catch them in the early stages.

Yes. I should have used it as an opportunity.

"Ron," I should have said, "have you started getting a thing about women's clothes like poor Gene Piscola?"

Because I'd just found out about *him* at the same time. The two things came together, like ham and eggs. All because of the girdle.

You see what happened was that sometime late February May Zetlinger stopped by to ask me if I had anything for the Thrift Store collection she was making.

"I don't suppose you have, really," she said, "with everything being nearly new and all."

And I said: "No, I'm afraid you're right, but no, hang on, I tell a lie, I've got some old clothes if they will do."

And she said: "Sure, as long as they're not really old, in rags."

And I said: "No, no of course not, I mean things that have gone out of fashion, and all that heavy woolen stuff we brought from England not knowing how good the central heating is over here. Come on upstairs and we'll take a look around."

So we did. And we'd collected quite an armful, when I remembered the girdle.

"Hold on," I said, "does *anybody* still wear the old-type stockings any more, because if they do there's a girdle in here that—"

Then I stopped. I'd been rummaging in the drawer.

"That's funny," I said. "It *was* here."

"Don't tell me you know where everything is, Pat, discarded clothes included?" said May.

She was laughing.

"Yes, I do," I said. "I'm very good at that."

And I am, it's one of the things I take a pride in, even things been lying in drawers or old steamer trunks years I know just where to put my hands on them.

"Well," she said, "I suppose it comes of there being only two of you. Now if—"

"Oh not *that* again!" I thought, getting a bit mad. "No but I don't like it when things just disappear!" I said aloud and not bothering to keep how annoyed I was out of my voice any more than she can be bothered to keep those six sodding kids out of everything she says.

So then she backed off a bit and had another go at laughing it off.

"You haven't let Gene Piscola loose up here recently, have you?" she said.

"Eh?" I said, looking up, still sore. "Gene Piscola? What's *he* got to do with it?"

"Don't you *know*, dear?" she said, sitting down on the bed and leaning over the bundle of old clothes she'd got in her arms already. "Aw now, come *on!*"

"No. Really." I wasn't so mad now. "*Gene Piscola?* Girdles?"

She was nodding, nodding, those glassy little eyes of hers, contact lenses I think, gleaming out of the wrinkles there like bits of broken bottles in dried mud.

Then she told me about Gene, and about how Julia had caught him one afternoon the summer before when she'd come home early from the dentist because he'd suddenly taken ill, the dentist I mean, and there was Gene struggling out of *her* panty-girdle, hose and all, but too late, and with lipstick still smeared on, and honestly, *laugh*, I thought I should wet myself there and then and I sat right down on the floor in front of the rummaged drawer and nearly split myself.

"Oh no!" I said, nearly crying. "Not Gene! Not Gene Piscola!"

I mean I was seeing him in my mind, tall, military, very serious, always crew-cut, always on about longhairs and what he'd do to them, and so *dignified*.

"Yes," said May. "And I might tell you there was nearly a divorce until he promised to go to a psychiatrist, her along with him, and get it straightened out. I thought they had too. . . . He *was* here at your party, wasn't he?"

Well then I sobered up a bit and shook my head and said, "No, forget it, May. I have a very good idea what's happened to anything I find missing these days, and unless I'm very much mistaken it was one of the perks that that cleaning woman we had, that Alice Whatsername, used to help herself to."

"Oh, *her!*" said May. "Well, yes, I'd forgotten you had her for a spell, yes."

And that was that.

Except that that wasn't *exactly* what had sobered me up, no. What had exactly crossed my mind just then was: "Oh dear, what if Ron's turned funny that way too?"

Because of course he had been acting strange for a long time, one way or another.

But almost as soon as I thought about it I dismissed it. What? Old Ron? Do that? Never. No. It was that Alice all right.

Which just shows you. You never can tell. Because here it is, in writing, proof, it was Ron all the time. Old Ron Fox had got it, even while I was puzzling over it with May. Locked away right there and then in the toolbox, I shouldn't wonder. Must have been. (I wonder where it is now?)

Anyway, at least it wasn't for anything kinky he wanted it. Thank God for that, at least.

Well.

Not *really* kinky.

Anyway, press on. It's late again, looks like being another midnight session. But never mind. Needs must. There's only one more day left before he's back, before the lock goes snap. Hardly that, because he'll be back early evening, should be. So press on, Pat. You can have a good lie-in on Saturday morning.

And the worst bit, the creepiest bit, is still to be copied out.

Poor sick Ron.

Never mind, we'll get you better.

So press on, Pat, don't let him down now, even if it means staying up till two or three again.

His Journal:
Entry Number 6

A note on Opportunity. In the Land of Opportunity, a note on Opportunity. Opportunity in relation to Bracknell's Law. To Determine the Relationship between the Factor of Opportunity and Bracknell's Law.

As one proceeds, it will be found that this note of jubilation, if not justified completely, is eminently forgivable.

Let me begin by quoting from my previous entry: "such natural advantages as casualness, anonymity, the camouflage of normalcy." This was in relation to Bracknell's Law, it will be recalled.

Well, now we can add Opportunity. Just, indeed, as we should have included it from the very beginning. For assuredly it looks like being a major element after all.

Strange, though, that it should never have been accorded its rightful significance until it absolutely thrust itself forward. Even in the early stages, the theoretical, the formulative stages, one would have thought that simple logic would have pointed it up. When all is said and done, those others—the casualness, anonymity, and so on—are merely contributory elements, the atoms that make up the molecule, important in themselves, granted, but not until they have been activated, brought into active cooperation. Yet Opportunity would seem to be that activating agent, that vital factor, galvanizing the others, giving them their true significance. Or to put it another way: Opportunity is the inflammatory or, better still, the *ignition* principle, causing the rest to catch light.

(But that last is an indulgence, a little joke, by which one is antici-pating, anyway.)

Stranger still is the fact that while there may be excuses for my having missed the point in the early theoretical stages (the history of science is full of instances of such blind spots), the principle, the im-portance of Opportunity as a factor, should not have been apparent after Experiment One. Wasn't that a blinding example of its efficacy, reaching into every detail, root and branch, down to the bonus, the grace note, of the shaking of the bottle? Like a poem in which the figures, phrases, words, even the very consonants and vowels, even the punctuation, are all in harmony with the theme.

And then they say that science and poetry are poles apart.

However, let me proceed.

Since making my last entry I had been carrying the problem around for several weeks. (Yes, "had been," not "have been"—because all this is by way of a preface, a preface to Experiment Two, its con-duct, and its absolutely terrific success. But patience. One must be patient when making the record, lest some vital, hitherto unnoticed factor should be overlooked, just as Opportunity—as a factor—was.)

I had been carrying the problem around for several weeks, then, but quite content, as noted in that entry, not impatient, allowing ideas all necessary time to germinate. I was going to kill a mugger and I knew I was capable of doing it and there was no shortage of muggers, heaven knows, so, as my adoptive compatriots would say: "No sweat."

Naturally, this attitude was reflected in my day-to-day affairs, I am thankful to say. No more outbursts at work, no more snapping at Pat. Thus cracks were beginning to close tightly again, scratches to heal, and everything to return to normal. (Not the dreadful hunted oppressive pre-Law norm, of course, but the happy post-Experiment-One norm we had been enjoying so deeply if for such a short period.)

Very well, then. Why not leave it at that, now that the balance had been restored?

A good question. But . . .

The balance had *not* been restored. Or, if it had, only in a tenuous probationary sort of way, and *only by virtue of intentions*. To aban-don those intentions would mean instantly to upset such balance as it was. Indeed, abandonment did just that, ever so slightly but ever so certainly, when the idea first occurred and I allowed myself to contemplate it even as a purely academic exercise.

So—reassured rather than dismayed by this (for didn't it act as further proof of the validity of the theory as a whole?)—I went on with the planning, slowly but surely, making progress to the point of finally deciding on the choice of gun.

A shotgun, preferably double-barreled, but single if circumstances so dictated. (I couldn't yet see how they might, apart from the fact that a double-barreled model might not be available at the time of inquiry, and that it is always advisable to cut confrontations of this type to the minimum. In other words, not to shop around, for fear of increasing the chances of being remembered.) To be sawed off short of course. But academic, anyway. And anyway, to proceed with the report, for now we are on the threshold of the experiment proper, I was all set to purchase the gun in West Virginia on my way home from a trip to southern Ohio, when opportunity intervened. One thing, in other words, led to another. Save that in this case the one thing was on a different plane from the other—as on or in a three-dimensional chessboard.

It was early March—a time that I have come quite to like over here, even though I've only been here two years. For although there is nothing spectacular about it (not like the later, dogwood period, for example, with spring in full burst), it is dramatic enough in one important transitional aspect: the change from the dreary dead gray-brown of the grass to bright, almost Irish, emerald green. Maybe also it is because that green doesn't have long to remain so bright, under the hot sun of a full American spring or summer, and is therefore all the more precious. One trusts that the author of that book didn't have such a *short-lived* Greening of America in mind! (Jesting again. One should really try to control it in a report of this kind. But then . . .)

Naturally, the best place to observe this pleasant phenomenon is not from a seat on a New Haven Railroad commuter train, but from the wheel of a car in the midwest, on roads that give one plenty of time to look around.

Thus, as I was driving back east from my last group of calls (I had worked my way around and up from Cincinnati, through Columbus, to Marion, making each my headquarters for a couple of days), I was happy. My prevalent mood had ensured good and fruitful contacts in the business field; the rains of the first few days had cleared the last streaks and stipples of snow; and for the latter half of the trip the weather had been clear, hazy in the early mornings and evenings, but sunny and quite warm in the afternoons. It was like that on this particular afternoon, as I speeded along secondary but near-deserted, fairly straight but pleasantly undulating roads, north of Mount Vernon, heading for Cambridge.

Cambridge was where I intended to spend the night (this was Thursday) preparatory to purchasing the gun in the morning, at Wheeling, and then proceeding home via the Ohio Turnpike and —interestingly and I hoped propitiously enough—Harrisburg. All in all, then, and in every possible way, the prospect was delightful, and somehow it was in keeping with the whole spirit of the enterprise that carefully stowed away in the trunk, alongside my cases and the fishing stool (the leather triangle forming a useful packing wedge at the moment), was a whole raft of plants, some of them in bud, some flowering already, in pots and shallow wooden boxes. I had seen them at a wayside store outside Marion and couldn't resist buying far more than I at first intended. For Pat, of course. God bless her. In the poetic context of the whole experiment, they were to make an excellent contribution.

Anyway, there it was. As I drove along that afternoon, admiring the look of the fields, it would not be too fanciful to say that there was a garden blossoming in the trunk and quiet joy in my heart.

It was as if I knew I was to meet him there, somewhere along that route to Cambridge, at a place where the roads should begin to veer more and the light to thicken, gray haze to blue haze to moon-streaked dusk with pockets of glossy blue-black. Pastoral, I think the word is. Something that touched me deeper than the daylit greenness, yet made me hum "Greensleeves" because somehow it —the quality of that dusk and darkness—was equally reminiscent of home. It was all I could do to remember to keep the car over to the right, and I shouldn't have been surprised to trap in the beams of my lamps, as I swept round the bends, something very English: a hedgehog, say, or a rural helmeted bobby, pedaling his way off duty.

Instead I saw the little man.

Standing at the side of the road, a jerry can at his feet, and waving frantically.

Elderly, scraggy, ordinary. No trouble. I pulled up, glad to be of service.

"Run out of gas?" I asked, out of the window.

My stopping seemed to make no difference to his agitation. He continued to hop from one foot to the other, and to turn his head jerkily after every hoarsely whispered word.

"No, no. I got it already. Listen, mister, you gotta help me!"

I sighed. Not "no trouble" after all. Some rustic idiot. But harmless.

"Well, if it's not gas—" I began.

But he was by the side of me now. He put out a claw, clutched my arm where it rested on the door, jerked his head again, away from me, toward the bend, beyond some bushes there, and said:

"Oh, Jesus! Just listen!"

At first, apart from his voice, I had heard nothing but the croaking chorus of frogs from some nearby pond. But now I could hear clumps, thumps—dull violent sounds that I couldn't place. And voices—raised but muffled.

"Them mothering angels! Them motherfucking angels!"

Had it not been for the sounds he'd drawn my attention to—increasing now in frequency—I should have been convinced of his insanity.

"Angels?"

"Motherfucking—oh Jesus excuse me, sir—Hell's Angels, yes."

I stiffened. I was getting the picture. I felt a tremor go through my body.

"My trailer," the man was saying, "the bastards, they've broken into my trailer. I ran out of gas, got a lift, got a lift back and let the truck go before I noticed nothin'. Then I see their bikes. Then I hear them. Jesus Christ, they're *wrecking* it, mister!"

"How—" I felt my voice clog. Oh yes. I have to admit it. Fear again. Just like that time in January. Same feeling exactly. "How many?"

"Five, six—maybe more, maybe more 'n one to a bike. For Christ's sake, mister—"

"Well, there's nothing—" again the clogging—"nothing we can do. Not against—"

"I *know* that, mister—what I'm saying—oh Jesus, hear that?—all I'm asking—you seen a highway patrol back there? A phone booth? Will you take me to the garage where—but oh Jesus, that's a fifteen-minute *drive*."

I was thinking. I couldn't just leave him to it. But of course there was no highway patrol along there, none that I had seen, anyway.

92

No phone booth, either—what did he think this was, Fifth Avenue? But there had been farms here and there, was one *here* in fact, nearby, judging from the light, a quarter of a mile, maybe less.

"Look. Over there," I told him. "That light. They'll have a phone. Farm. Probably. Your best bet's there."

He seemed to notice it for the first time. He clutched my arm again.

"Yeah—sure—good. Maybe some hands, someone—yeah. You wanna drive me there, right now?"

He was already making for the passenger door.

Well. I didn't know. Could it be some kind of fancy stick-up? Accomplices. Get me down a dirt road.

All at once there was nothing pastoral-English about the scene any more.

I reached out, but only to flip shut the lock.

Then I got out.

"Look," I said, "I'm not sure where the road *is*. Why don't you head straight across the field on foot? It'll be quicker. You could be there by the time—"

"Sure, sure. Could you come with me, though? I—"

"No," I said. What, and leave the car here unguarded? Next in line for treatment? No. "I'll stick around, take a look at the bikes, get some kind of identification."

He was already on his way, gasping his thanks over his shoulder with one jerk of the head, groaning "Jesus Christ" with the next.

Well, fair enough. I'd meant what I'd said. I wasn't going to fall for any trap and I wasn't going to leave my own property exposed, trap or no trap. But I was rapidly becoming convinced anyway, both by his manner and the noises off, and I sympathized. Hell's Angels I detest. Always have. I'm right with Gene Piscola there. Vermin. So anything I could do, within reason, I would.

I walked to the bend, taking care to tread softly, keeping to the grassy shoulder. And as I rounded it the clumping and thumping became quite loud, mixed with laughter—muffled laughter—harsh, ugly, strident and loud but muffled, mingled with the clumps and crashes, a part of them. There suddenly came the sound of breaking glass, also part of the rest.

The trailer loomed surprisingly close, pale, lit up, close enough for me to see how wildly it was rocking. The car was ahead, screened by it, but on my side I could see the gleaming tangle of bikes, parked on the shoulder.

Hell's Angels, all right. High intimidating steerlike handlebars. Pennants. Gadgetry. Bristling like Flying Fortresses—threatening even when unmanned.

I suddenly felt a lurch of fear again.

What if one of them should come out now and see me snooping around?

Then, just as suddenly, there came the tidal wave of rage.

The crucible suddenly flowered to the boil, spat, expanded, spilled. The addition of rage to fear. We added to the solution 1 mg. of rage. . . .

Then, as quickly, it subsided, the flowering shrinking, the surface calming, not cooling, note—*calming*. No, not cooling. Hot, quiescent, deadly.

Thus the sense of Opportunity was distilled.

A sense of Ripeness, Fitness, Inevitability.

Informed by Urgency—but a confident Urgency.

Why not? I thought.

I may even have shrugged, I felt so seethingly calm. Dry ice.

I went back quickly to the jerry can, which he had left by my car. As I approached it I checked quickly to make sure I was still wearing my gloves. I picked up the jerry can. I unscrewed the cap, ready. I hastened back to the trailer. And as I approached it, I checked quickly to make sure the matchbook was still in my left-hand pocket.

At the side of the trailer I took stock.

Noises, voices. Not so many clumps. Be careful.

"Hey, man, leave something for *me!*"

"Hey, lookit! Take a look at *this!*"

"*Dirty* old man!"

Every window seemed to have been smashed and that was good. They had closed the door behind them, probably at first for greater security against passing cars. Better.

I decided on the window nearest the door. I trusted there was no other door. The windows were rather large, of course, but then they had smashed them, giving them jagged, lethal—or at least awkward —borders of broken glass, on which the drapes had been caught as they fluttered. Splendid.

Again I hoped nobody would take it into his head to come out.

94

But this time the reaction to the thought was not panic, simply annoyance at potential frustration.

Anyway, they were too busy.

Someone called out from the far end:

"Hey! Here's the stove. How about some coffee, men?"

There was a dull clumping toward that end. Jackboots. Crushers of innocent fingers. Kickers of law-abiding skulls. Crowding into the kitchen. Away from this door. Much obliged. Much obliged I was for this help, this sign, this sub-opportunity, this indication that all was well, that all was fitting, everything clicking, parts of a poem.

I glanced around.

Nothing. No headlamps sweeping the sky.

The little man would barely have reached the farm. Maybe just stammering his explanations to some slow-tumbling suspicious hick.

The frogs were rising to a crescendo seemingly encouraging. I thought of a Cup Final crowd back home at Wembley, with a winning goal in the offing.

I lifted the jerry can to the window by the door, and tilted it sharply, angling the tilt toward the door. It giggled as it poured free and I felt like giggling along with it. But I could have wished it would pour faster. I wondered how long to wait before tossing in the match. The matchbook and one freed match were already in my left hand. Could I wedge the damned can and leave both hands free? Would they smell it and twig first? A nice problem. Then someone called:

"Hey! You guys empty the gas tank or some—?"

And then it happened.

One of them must have been smoking.

Or maybe lighting the stove.

There was a tremendous whoosh, a crump, a flash. I felt my hair being whipped as I jumped back. Then the furnace, the immediate instant furnace, a scream, screams.

Nobody, but no *body*, would ever get out of that.

I turned and ran for the car.

If anyone happened by now, stopped me, caught me, I had my story. I'd been to snoop, as promised. One of them emerged, saw me, snatched the jerry can, intending to fire the trailer, but got caught instead. How about the Angel outside with the can? Brave Angel. Got to hand it to them. Guts. But no sense. Went into save. Stayed to broil. Fiery Angel.

I told myself yes, it would hold. Who would think that a passing salesman/technical consultant, eminently respectable, could have done this thing? Bracknell's Law in operation here. Safe enough. Not even *my* trailer.

But don't listen to the screams, I told myself.

Maybe there weren't any after those first, after rounding the bend. But don't listen anyway. Not your bag. Not interested. No gloating. Scientific. No sadism. None of *that* craziness. Bracknell's Law. Logical. Constructive. Cleansing.

Even now I could get carried away.

Anyway. I jumped into the car P.D.Q. There were still no signs from the direction of the farm. I started the engine. I felt safe. Now I was merely driving along, approaching the place for the first time. Unsuspecting. The glow was just a farmer's rubbish fire, as far as I was concerned. Yes.

But no.

I couldn't do it. I just couldn't go ahead and pass it.

So I swung around. I headed back the way I'd come. And with every revolution of the wheels I began to feel good. With every turn, the realization of what I had done got clearer.

Wasn't this better than any mugger?

Four, five, six of *those* bastards?

A mugger does have a purpose, an economic reason, a rationale. Given an awareness of that, one can make plans to avoid muggers. But these swine, no. Random in their violence, they had perished by random violence. Perfect. World that much cleaner.

That is the way my thoughts were running. In fragments, but hard, purposeful, like bullets. Meanwhile, deeper than thought, at the endocrine levels, I could feel the balance forming, taking definition, the true balance, no longer merely its foreshadow. I felt it as a slow surging, a steady seeping, and it was great.

All the time in the world now. No need for gun, no need for elaborate program.

I think I sang out aloud.

"Greensleeves" again, but with a lilt.

I was still humming it when I checked in at the motel near Marion. Next morning I would go back to that wayside flower place and order more. As many again. I would say I'd been thinking it over in the motel and had so decided. They would remember me, all right.

They did. And of course they assumed I'd been in the area all the time. It was alibi enough. Not that it mattered. Just another grace note. One of our little extras. Bracknell Experimentation tries harder. Secret of our success.

And success it was. One has only to study the following report—a selection from many. There was no problem about finding a paper with it in this time.

Her Journal:
Entry Number 10

No. Too long to write it out tonight. Too tired. More tired than I expected. Those poor boys. Because that was real of course, there was that blaze, it's all in the report. And what I mean is it's bad enough just thinking about such a thing, just making it up, it's sick enough, but basing it on some real Tragedy makes it worse, and writing it all down, all his words about it, all that thought he must have put into it, suddenly it makes me feel dead tired, more tired than just the lateness.

Something will have to be done for him, poor lamb. No doubt about that. But what? Too tired now. Besides, still a lot to do tomorrow, more news reports, more words from Ron, and what words some of them. Must get them all down before he comes home.

Just this though also. Even the flowers. Those gorgeous flowers so many some I still have, had never anyone given me so many. Beginning of another golden period, even more confident, cheerful (don't go by the way he writes, he was much looser, more relaxed, full of real fun, never lost for a joke, sharp as a needle, beat some of these American men at their own game), but of course this changes it. Knowing it was all sickness, like TB patients who're supposed to look blooming but they're all rotting inside, well so it must have been with Ron. And now he's killed those flowers, now they're blighted, even the ones that died anyway they still flowered in my mind but not any more. Oh dear. Oh Ron, whatever shall we do about you? Whatever will become of us? But keep your chin up, your Pat is on to it now, she'll work something out, goodnight God bless my darling.

Her Journal:
Entry Number 11

What a day to oversleep! What a time for Madame Zetlinger to come about the Thanksgiving Ball arrangements, thought she'd never go! And me in all my muck, no housework done, what will Ron think tonight, well never mind. First things first. Will skip lunch, will work straight through, should be time so long as no one else comes visiting. Good job I haven't lost knack though, still very fast, only hope it isn't too much of a scrawl, please excuse scrawl.

Now. Where was I oh yes.

The report. Can skip a bit here and there maybe, the blah blah blah, save time on that, can always check in the library files, just so long as you get Ron's own words down every single one, even one could be important to an expert never mind what you think, Pat. And maybe come to think every single word of report too, never know which of them triggered ideas off in the poor lamb's head, yes, mustn't forget that. Anyway.

First the report then Ron's next entry, comments on the report and that, there's where it's important.

TRAILER INFERNO TRAGEDY

FIVE DEAD

Police are investigating the deaths near here of five youths, Carl Schroeder, Wilson P. Ayres, Andrew Paris, Jackson Carlile, and Wayne Rodetsky, all of Pittsburgh, who were trapped by flames while allegedly vandalizing a trailer belonging to Aaron Schumaker, 60, of St. Louis. Mr. Schumaker, a retired silversmith, had only last week commenced the six months' touring vacation that he and his late wife had been planning for years. He was on his way to look up old friends in Cambridge when he ran out of gas on Scenic Route 586. Leaving the trailer parked at the roadside, he thumbed a lift to a garage seven miles away, and on returning with the gasoline discovered that his trailer had been broken into and that the alleged offenders were still inside. "One look at the bikes they had left on the shoulder told me that these were Hell's Angels or persons of that ilk," Mr. Schumaker explained. "So I immediately took steps to secure help." A passing motorist whom he flagged down suggested that he telephone for police assistance from the nearby Generis Birch farm, and it was while Mr. Schumaker was doing so that the conflagration occurred.

Missing Witness

One theory under consideration is that on emerging from the trailer after inflicting more damage than intended, the youths found the gasoline and got the idea to fire the trailer to cover their traces, not realizing the high combustibility of the fumes in a confined space as they splashed the gasoline about. "All it needed was for one of them to be smoking," said Sheriff Willis R. Everett. Questioned by our reporter, Mr. Schumaker said: "Regarding the man I spoke with, he just vanished. He told me he would stick around while I was telephoning, but when the kids started coming out the first time I guess he got scared and drove off, leaving the jerry can there for them to find. I don't blame him, either. How could he have known they would do this foolish thing, anyway?"

"Tragic Event"

The sheriff is anxious to trace the missing witness, saying that every shred of evidence, no matter how apparently insignificant, would be invaluable in helping complete the picture of the "tragic event." According to Mr. Schumaker's description, the man is very tall, at least 6 ft. 3 in., fair, in his twenties, and speaks with a Bostonian accent. He was driving a blue Oldsmobile sedan. "I admit

I am a bit hazy about the details," said Mr. Schumaker today. "You have to remember it was dark at the time and I had other things on my mind. But the Boston accent and the make of car I am pretty sure of."

Agent Robert T. Blakey of the Bureau of Criminal Investigation and Identification arrived on the scene early this morning to assist the sheriff's department in its investigation. When asked to comment on his being called in, he said it was a routine matter in all such cases and did not necessarily indicate any suspicion of homicide. Sheriff Everett added to this that it was only natural that every possibility should be investigated. Pressed further, he conceded that the victims' known association with the Hell's Angels cult did give rise to the possibility of gang warfare, or "inter-chapter rivalry" as he expressed it. "It just might be that this is the culmination of a vendetta," he said. "If that should have any substance, you may be sure the investigation will spread far beyond this county."

His Journal:
Entry Number 7

God bless you, Aaron Schumaker!

I read this report just half an hour ago and I couldn't help it, the words sprang to my lips like music, like the carol.

God bless you, Aaron Schumaker!

On my way back via Harrisburg (it was so worth taking a little time off from the Turnpike), I made my pilgrimage to the shrine of Otis Newstrander and oh, how I wish I'd known your name then. Newstrander, Schumaker: one a victim, the other a beneficiary: the two poles of Bracknell's Law, chiming like a pair of bells, one a warning, one rejoicing, Newstrander, Schumaker. I would have thrown a flower out onto the grass for you too, Schumaker, had I known, a small token of our esteem, and assuring you of our best attention at all times, etc., etc.

But no. The truth. It was not just for the sound of your name that I felt like singing, Mr. Schumaker. No. But for your tidings, Mr. Schumaker.

Because although I had counted on your being confused, unable to give a coherent description, I never dared hope for this.

This is so much better.

This is priceless.

I haven't had a drink all day, haven't needed one, but, honestly, since reading the report I have felt slightly but definitely but delightfully tipsy.

"Six foot three *at least*."

A benison for one who barely touches six, in circumstances like these. Probably because he was so small, compounded by his acute feeling of vulnerability at the time.

"Fair."

Too much, too much! For heaven's sake, where did you get that notion from, Mr. Schumaker, in the dark and all? At night all cats are fair? Something to do with stature again and the feeling of vulnerability hitting him where he lives racially? Not to worry, Mr. Schumaker. The jackboots got their comeuppance this time, what? (I liked the name of that Carl Schroeder, too, but for different, opposite reasons. I hope his coming first in the list meant he was the leader, or should we say führer? Was he one of those that flaunt Iron Crosses, I wonder? Was he first in there, bent on wrecking the poor little bastard's retirement with a dozen swings of the boot and the tire iron? If so, I trust—I most sincerely trust—that he was the last to die.)

God bless you, Mr. Schumaker.

He blessed you this time, all right. He sent the right man your way this time. Is it this tipsiness or do I really read between the lines a certain satisfaction in your soul, Mr. Schumaker? Indeed, can it be—oh heavens, this really would be too much!—but can it be that you suspect the truth, that your description has been *deliberately* misleading?

But "Bostonian accent"—really!

I suppose to a midwesterner who'd never been around, the Englishness might come out that way. After all, didn't the lady at Love Field who sold me the fishing stool say, to my reply to her question was I from Germany, "Well, I could tell you weren't from around these parts"? She was Texan, of course, but—well, I suppose it figures. Bostonian. And it does go well with the subject. Baked beans—baked goons—oh well.

And finally, the car. How anyone could mistake a black Buick for a blue Olds is beyond me. I have heard that the police get this all the time, complain right bitterly about it, but even so, when it happens to oneself it does seem odd. Yet then again he was a worried little chap. He certainly did have other things on his mind.

God bless you anyway, Mr. Schumaker. May nothing again, ever any more, you dismay.

As for Sheriff Earp and Agent Ness or whatever they're called (*theirs* are names that don't interest me), all I can say is "Right on, men!" I can just see how keen they are to clear the fair name of their county, their state, and if they can pin it on another bunch of Hell's Angels how nice it would be for everyone concerned. What a truly *epic* poem!

But this is just romantic froth, the spurt from the victory bottle, the ejaculation of success. The true results will show themselves in the deeper currents of personality, at less spectacular levels, and we shall see. But if what happened after Experiment One is anything to go by, just think of the results of this. Five to one? Or is the ratio more complex?

We'll see. Stand by for later reports, when the dust (and soot) has settled. One should have regained some measure of detachment before too long.

Hey, but right now, Mr. Schumaker . . .

God bless you, huh?

His Journal:
Entry Number 8

I have deliberately waited for six weeks or so to elapse in order to ensure the attainment of that desired level of detachment referred to at the end of the last entry.

Indeed, looking over that outpouring, one cannot help but feel somewhat ashamed, and wonder whether or not to expunge it from the record. Alarmed, too, for it is in such euphoric states, one feels, that there lies the maximum danger of self-betrayal. That much is obvious. It obtains in all walks of life, all projects and predicaments. But in *this* particular set of circumstances the danger is especially great.

The danger is especially great because the temptations to give one's euphoria free rein are especially strong. For consider:

This experiment has become a cause célèbre. Quite unlike the other, this one hit, as they say, the headlines. This one made the television screen. This one did not have to be rooted out from a mess of local or regional news sheets, days after the event. One is not *one-self* belittling the importance of that first experiment. Of course not. As the first small but essential and tremendously difficult step, its importance simply cannot be overestimated. It was in fact of immeasurably greater importance than the second. But from the point of view of the unwitting observer, of some two hundred million unwitting observers, of, indeed, some two hundred million *plus* unwitting observers (for this is the typical sensational news item seized on so avidly and equally typically by the world's press as being so typically sensationally American), it has loomed large.

People were talking about it right from the start.

It cropped up in all contexts.

It cropped up in quiet domestic conversation, in the by-the-way exchanges on trains and buses, in the non-shop marginal exchanges at work, and, this being America—or should one say this being Palmers Point?—inevitably at parties.

Secret delights; secret desires; public danger.

Secret delights in knowing that one—one's mere self—was responsible for this hullabaloo, and that one, and only oneself, held the key to an incident that was baffling millions and completely misleading millions more.

Secret desires to correct, to interject, to draw attention to a fact here or introduce an overlooked point there that would pull up the owners of the fatuously working mouths in front of one, pull them up and straighten them up, their fatuity finally and convincingly proven.

The danger of succumbing needs no stressing. Under the force of the original euphoria, it is a wonder that I didn't succumb. Yet this is hardly cause for self-congratulation. Rather for a certain measure of unease. For such euphoria is tantamount to being drunk and there are times when one wonders (as after a boozy evening) just how much one did give away, even obliquely. There are certain seeds, winged or parachuted, that drift laterally for ages, for miles, before settling and germinating. So why not these mental seeds in such circumstances as those under discussion?

Let us review those circumstances, then, applying a microscope to some, a spectrograph to others, a sample here, a sweep there. It is the least one can do.

The public reactions may be divided into two main categories: theories and opinions.

THEORIES

Of the people with whom one discussed the matter, or whom one overheard discussing the matter, the majority—let us say some seventy-five percent at a rough estimate—agreed with that theory propounded in the newspaper clipping appended above: that the youths were hoist with their own petard. Foremost of those contenders were: Pat herself, who expressed or reiterated it with much sighing and head-shaking and piteous looks (so like her, good sweet Pat, whose views one respects even in the act of secretly mocking them); and Gene Piscola; our upright, hawklike upholder of all things truly American (in his view, crew cuts, apple pie, and American womanhood). *His* reiteration, confirmation, sealing and settling and guaranteeing of the theory was delivered in quite the opposite mode from Pat's, however: in tones of much quiet jubilation. This really comes under the head of *Opinions*, one supposes, but it is mentioned here to indicate that where belief in theories obtains, vast moral gulfs may appear between individual adherents without the fact being at all apparent. Yet another little service performed by the application of Bracknell's Law. However . . .

The next largest group of theorists—one might put it at ten percent of the whole sample—inclined to the hypothesis put forward by the sheriff (see clipping above) that the "tragedy" occurred as the result of a vendetta with a rival gang. Strangely enough, the adherents to this notion were mainly women, with a sprinkling of milquetoast men like Roger Townsend in the Accounts Department. And here again there were indications of split motivation, some of the women relishing the idea for its drama (the gang-warfare element—husky young studs battling it out no doubt because of some dispute over a girl or girls); and others, the more pacific-minded and shrinking of them, including all the men in this category, because they would rather believe that such a (to them) horrible thing was perpetrated solely by horrible people and not by anyone remotely resembling themselves. One can imagaine with what glee I detected such tendencies! However, again . . .

The next group, almost as numerous as the last-mentioned—let us say nine percent of the whole—might be designated the typical Eastern Flip Cynic Fringe. Their theory—not reiterated but seemingly original, though it had a certain foreshadowing even in that early news report, a between-the-lines projection as it were—posited a redneck lynching element. The sheriff of course was covering up. The mention of a vendetta was a deliberate red herring. If there *was* a vendetta it was not between rival packs of greasers, hell no, but between any pack of greasers and the God-fearing, law-abiding, silently majoring rustics of Ohio.

That, I note, brings the tally to ninety-four percent, and again I stress the roughness of the estimate. The grouping fluctuates anyway, as in all such cases, as so-called fresh evidence comes to light and new official theories are propounded. But, whatever the exact percentages, two further categories must be mentioned, two ultra-minority reports, as one might say.

Three people—three individuals, note, not three percent of the whole—of my acquaintance subscribe, albeit tentatively (for these are the *thoughtful* men, the quiet thoughtful types, who always seem to be puffing at pipes even if they are in fact non-smokers), to the belief that Mr. Schumaker himself did it, that he came back and, in a fit of rage at finding the vandals at work, fired the trailer there and then. Anyone who had seen Mr. S., even on television let alone in the flesh, would know that this was nonsense. One sees his big brown dolefully watering eyes and hears his slow broken voice and knows at once that he is of the Pat variety—soft-hearted, sincere—someone who truly would have preferred the vandals to have gotten away with the firing of his property (he himself belongs to the seventy-five per-cent in this) rather than have lost their lives in such a way. But your thoughtful man, your quiet thoughtful pipe-puffer, is nearer the cynical fringe than he would ever admit. He rejects such notions about Mr. Schumaker's innocence as "emotionally based" and that, for him, means shaky if not downright erroneous. He further avows that Mr. Schumaker's reacting in the way propounded would be "logical" (and that is another sacred cow), quite overlooking the fact that the fit of rage on which the "logical" argument is based is arrantly emotional itself. Charlie Raybourn is foremost of this muddled minority. Naturally.

Which leaves the final theory, considered by many but quickly re-jected, and held firmly by only one person of my acquaintance: literally a minority of one (or, as some Americans might consider it, a minority of one half). I refer to an elderly black shoeshine boy at Grand Central, the other week, who, noticing my interest in the latest spate of theorizing about the experiment, in an item in the *New York Times* (the incident having sparked off a number of Vengeance Rides in that area of Ohio, a series of mobile riots on the part of other motorcycle gangs), lifted up a grizzled head and mur-mured:

"Now me, if I was that sheriff, I'd be looking real hard for that missing witness, yes sir."

I nearly dropped the paper with shock.

"Hah?"

He tapped the folded-down half of the paper with the tip of his brush, scratching the headline.

"This Hell's Angels affair. You know what *I* figure? I figure the cops should be working on the missing-witness angle. The man with the Boston accent."

"How come?" I said, squeezing as much of New York as I could into my voice.

"Stands to sense." He chuckled as he began slapping my left shoe with his rag. "Some *purretty* strange characters come from that place. I been there. Remember the Strangler?"

I laughed. I suddenly felt enormously relieved.

But the fifty-cent tip I gave him was for his instinctive acumen, to say nothing (for one must be honest) of throwing the pipe-smokers into such high and unflattering relief.

Such then is one's breakdown—very rough—of the theories at large. It will be noted that there are zero "Don't Knows" in this sample survey. But that is because one's silent canvass took place in Palmers Point and New York City, where nobody dares be without a theory of some kind on any subject, it seems.

OPINIONS

Much concerning opinion has been interspersed with the breakdown on theories, of course. Yet some record under this head is worth making if only because opinion has a tendency to cut across the boundaries of theory, as in the case of Pat's sympathy with the victims and Gene Piscola's gloating over them. In this respect, the general breakdown would appear to be almost fifty-fifty: i.e., about half the people discussing the matter being of the opinion that the boys deserved all they got, and the other half averring that the nature of their death eclipsed any consideration of deserts, just or otherwise. As we have seen, at the outer ends of the spectrum we have Pat on the one hand:

"Those poor, poor boys! They couldn't have stood a chance."

And Gene on the other:

"Serve the little bastards right! I'm not saying I'd have fanned the flames any, but I sure as hell wouldn't have shed any tears."

The two quotations are taken from an exchange at the Hunters', about a week later, while the affair was still—pardon the expression—red-hot news. What followed is worth examining in some detail.

"Aw, come on!" said Charlie Raybourn. "You can't mean that,

Gene!" (He knew damned well that Gene could mean it, and would insist even more strongly that he did, when challenged thus, so providing him, Charlie Raybourn, with an adversary who, by contrast, would allow him, Charlie Raybourn, to sound like Clarence Darrow and Bertrand Russell combined.) "To say that something serves somebody right is like saying that that something is a fitting punishment for whatever they've done."

"Yes, well, so it is," said Gene, nibbling, straightening his shoulders, glancing around for moral support.

"You mean you would actually send vandals to the *chair?*" said Harry Zetlinger, not caring a hoot really, but ever ready to join in a bout of Gene-baiting. "You'd have them fry *electrically?*"

"Certainly not," said Gene, standing up straighter than ever, and carefully laying his bourbon down on the edge of a sideboard to emphasize his high seriousness. "I didn't say that."

"But you—"

"All I said"—Gene was raising his voice, but firmly, authoritatively, back in the Army again, overriding a subordinate on the brink of insubordination—"was"—he glanced around, obviously glad to see a crowd gathering, unaware of the nudges of some of the women, mistaking the sparkle in their eyes for admiration—"that if they choose to do such damn-fool things, they must expect to take the consequences."

"The consequences being a little sneaky lynching on the side, huh?" said Harry Zetlinger (one of the Flip Fringe party).

"Who said anything about lynching?" said Gene, smirking a little at this chance to score. "I happen to believe that it occurred quite naturally, that this thing blew back in their faces."

"An act of God, huh?" said Charlie Raybourn, his eyes in green slits, not happy that Gene should have had that chance to score, but ready now to cut him down.

"If you want to put it that way," said Gene, shrugging. "Yes. Why not?"

"Isn't that being a bit straight-laced, Gene?" said Brenda Hunter, who was half drunk and had a wild hysterical laugh belling up at the back of her throat.

Now this was a direct reference to a rather distasteful rumor that was going the rounds concerning Gene. This is not the place to retail such trash. Suffice it to say that the reference had its effect.

"Excuse me?" Gene looked puzzled.

So did some of the others. Others again began to snigger. But Charlie and Harry and most of the men were in a debating mood, feeling heavy, wanting to show off their intellectual strength, and Brenda was frowned out of court.

"You believe God would approve, then?" said Ralph Hunter, more to blot out his wife's slip than to advance the argument, and giving her a glance that suggested a little roasting might not come amiss later, in his own home.

"Well—some people do still believe in Hell—sure, yes."

"Jesus Christ!" said Harry Zetlinger, rolling his eyes around. "Would you ever believe in this day and—"

"I happen to believe that it wasn't an accident," said Charlie, giving first Harry, then me, a hard look.

(*Stop-Action Analysis*: Here one must pause and recollect one's momentary uneasiness. His look at Harry was understandable: a chairman's plea for correct debating manners. But why the look at me? Almost at once, I realized it was nothing more nor less than the old look, one that he'd been in the habit of throwing at me often during the early period of our stay here: the patron/sponsor look, follow-my-lead-and-you'll-be-all-right, with even a hint of the boss look, back-me-up-or-else. Occasionally, despite the changed circumstances, he will still, absentmindedly, revert to it. Thus it must have been on this occasion.)

"I happen to believe that the trailer owner himself might have had something to do with it," Charlie rumbled on. "But leaving the specifics aside for the minute. Suppose it was not an accident. Suppose it was an act of revenge, or retaliation, or simply a too heavy-handed attempt at self-defense, even an attempt to scare them. Do you *still* think they deserved *that*?"

"Well," said Gene, with a flash of logic that surprised most of us, "some of that you've just mentioned, Charlie, why, it does come under the heading of accident."

Charlie stiffened.

"Let's not split hairs, Gene, huh? Let's not try and wriggle out of *this* one"—a flicker for the ladies, not lost on them, his revenge for having had the loophole spotted, a dirty fighter under all that sweet reasonableness, Charles P. Raybourn. "Let's—what?" (Innocently, looking around him.)

Some of the women had started giggling. Gene had gone red around the ears and had picked up his bourbon and was drinking it with his eyes fixed hard on Charlie. Ralph Hunter, sensing trouble, suddenly turned to me.

"Hey, Ron, *you're* the guy to have all the inside dope on this thing. Hey, folks, hold it! Why argue about the *possible* causes when there's a guy here can put the record straight right away?"

(*Stop-Action Analysis:* Another bad moment. But one that quickly passed at the sight of Hunter's open expression, clown grin, appealing eyes, and next remarks, which came tumbling out with the urgency of *his* predicament.)

"Ron, you were in Ohio that week, weren't you?"

"Aha!"

"Why, sure!"

Some of the others were rallying around their host, peeling away from the still-glaring Gene and Charlie, helping to lower the temperature, save the party. Now, once again, I became the instrument for that vital social instinctive reaction, and once again I was equal to the demand.

"Curse you for a meddling jackanapes!" I snarled, with a Karloffian lisp. "I had hoped you would none of you remember. But—ha!—you'll not take me alive!"

With that, I drained my vodka martini as if it had been cyanide, then heaved long rasping gasps and glared around.

But I'd been overdoing it. Again the euphoria.

Did anyone notice?

For of course, even in jest, my own guilt hadn't been in question.

"Which one is that speaking to us?" Ralph was saying. "The Schroeder kid or one of the others?"

Then I realized, remembered.

I straightened up, shook off the monster-at-bay role, pretended to ponder.

"Well, all kidding apart, Ralph"—and that in itself got a few expected danger-deflecting laughs—"I do believe I sneezed again at the time it all must have been happening—"

"Oh, Ron, *please!*" said Pat. "It's not a laughing matter."

"I should think not," said Charlie Raybourn, glad at last not to be the focus of unpleasantness, thankful at having been saved from his own nasty inclinations. "Pat just doesn't know who it is getting into bed with her when you get home from these trips."

There was a big laugh for that. Someone behind me was explaining to a puzzled visitor to Palmers Point a joke I had made at a previous party, about how my body had been invaded as I slept by the spirit of a recently dead man. (Newstrander, in fact.) Pat turned and went over to the food table.

"Well, exactly which one it was this time," I said, "I couldn't say. All I know is that I had a sudden urge to dress up in black leather and jackboots the other morning. And yesterday I caught myself wanting to smash up the men's room at work."

With everyone but Pat it went down big, my contribution that evening.

But as we have noted, it could have turned out otherwise.

For the euphoria was still very much at work then, and the temptations were commensurately great. Because note this:

Whatever the theories or opinions, there was underlying them all a deep general satisfaction. It was there even in the eyes of most of those who professed pity. (Pat always excepted, God bless her.) To know that one was the cause of such universal satisfaction gave one a great feeling, naturally. *But it was greater still—vastly greater—when one reminded oneself of the fact that one had been capable of doing what so many others could only—and that very secretly—*feel *like doing.*

His Journal:
Entry Number 9

How different everything looks when that inner balance is restored and reestablished.

One thinks of the contrast between this May and last.

Palmers Point really is quite a pleasant place. Suburban, yes, but old suburban, well established itself, well treed, well shrubbed. One would hardly think this was a high-density neighborhood at this time of the year. Hardly rural, of course, but pleasantly blurred in the corners and outlines, with—and let us not forget this—the ocean no more than the proverbial stone's throw (given a good catapult) away.

And now, with the dogwood, a delight.

Strange that it wasn't so apparent last year.

Even Pat is beginning to feel more settled. We were discussing this last night, and although she still hankers after the bright lights of New York (and one must remember that she has to remain here all day and every day), there is not the same sense of urgency.

"If you're happy, so am I, Ron."

Well, "happy" is hardly the word.

"It's a question of building up a charge, Pat," I began to tell her.

"Charge?"

She thought I was referring to money. I decided perhaps it might get us both into water that was too deep if I proceeded. I changed the subject. Suffice it that she benefits by association, induction, reflection. Such, after all, is the essence of Bracknell's Law, its obliqueness. Like billiards in a way. No direct shot ever. One hits one ball to pocket quite another. Oh well . . .

But I think she was satisfied with my argument on more orthodox, more obvious lines.

"If we wait until my next promotion—which shouldn't be very long—we'll not only have more funds, Pat, we'll also have more time together."

"Oh?"

"Why, yes. You see, the next step will keep me in the office more. Fewer trips. After all, New York really isn't much fun for a woman on her own. I mean a wife whose husband is away anything up to two or three weeks in the month. Not when she's madly in love with him."

"Bighead!" she said at that.

But she was laughing.

For she *is* madly in love with me. That has been another by-product of the Law, another side-effect of the balance. It is almost the same as the first years of our marriage. Better. Because of course more firmly founded.

And I meant it when I said the next promotion won't be long. Not with the way I'm feeling. Not with the way things have been shaping. Nothing seems to stand in my way these days. I mean even including the unexpected twists and turns, outside one's direct control.

"Must be something to do with your stars," Sylvia Raybourn said to me the other night, more than a trifle wistfully, I thought.

I winked at her. I felt impish. "Aren't you forgetting the supernatural help I'm getting?"

"The what?"

"Otis P. Newstrander," I said.

"Oh, him!"

"Yes, him. He got to know a lot of useful business secrets in his job," I said. "And since he's passed them on to me, it's surprising how many doors fall open."

"Well, just remember what happened to *him*," said Charlie, sourly. "And anyway, I thought he'd been superseded by the Schroeder kid."

I changed the subject. No sense in driving a thing into the ground. I said no, all kidding aside, I'd never looked back since joining the Beach Club. Made a new man of me.

"But that was only two weeks ago," said Sylvia, chiding a little, wanting to get back to the supernatural, or to astrology at least.

"Beach Club!" snorted Charlie, seeing his chance to restore some of his own balance. "Why you've chosen that crummy outfit when there's half a dozen of us all raring to sponsor you for the Yacht Club beats me, Ron."

"It's the dues," said Pat, before I could give her the keep-quiet look. And of course that did restore the Raybourn balance, such as it is.

"Well, they *are* pretty high," he said.

"It's the dues in conjunction with the returns," I said. "We could afford them all right, Charlie, you know that. But why pay all that when we've no kids to make fullest use of the amenities . . . ?"

Such is the piddling ebb and flow of suburban balance sheets. A year ago an exchange like that would have left me feeling itchy, annoyed with myself as well as with Pat. No doubt we would have fought over it the minute we were alone.

But not this time. It seems as if nothing can shake me off course now, as if we're all set for a long steady smooth glide downstream. All in all, a feeling of deep abiding peace and stability, and if ever it should flag (one gets physically tired at times, naturally), why then there is always the news to give a boost, reminding one of the unique, untouchable springs of one's power. For the incident is still alive, still meriting journalistic attention, especially now that this self-styled Greasers' Lawyer has appeared on the scene to stir things up.

Imagine.

One could feel annoyed really. A side-effect of Bracknell's Law *not* exactly welcomed. A free gift of rich publicity to a shark like *that*. Giving press conferences in riding leathers and his hair shoulder length. All too reminiscent of some of those lawyers snuffling around the fringes of student riots.

But there you are. Every cause, good or bad, is bound to attract such parasites and opportunists. One mustn't grudge it them for fear of losing focus on the prime objective. Bastards, though, all the same. Maybe the application of a little of Bracknell's Law to one or two of *them* . . .

Enough. One is tending toward foolishness again. This double damned habit of flipness is so catching. So forget the parasites, the negatives. Concentrate on the positives: the passing on of the fruits of one's power to the humble, the meek, the victimized. The job of

116

moral cleansing, the unexpected proffering of redress, the giving of hope, a glint here, a glimmer there, until it becomes a bright steady blaze. All done by oblique strokes. Triggered by acts of devotion that will in turn trigger others. Tiny switches relaying megatons.

One has been thinking about the Assassins. Not the crude monsters of pulp fiction and comic book, but the original cult. One remembers reading a serious article about them, and portions of it keep floating back. Basically a deeply religious, highly moral cult. Nothing personal about it. No pandering to simple blood lust, no giving in to thirst for personal revenge. Quite gentle really. Quite detached. Like Bracknell's Law. No killing of trespassers against oneself (but then of course no forgiving, either). Simply a transference, the obliqueness: I shall kill the unclean ones, those who have similarly trespassed, but against others. *Was* this it? Or is this pure Bracknellism superimposing itself?

No matter. The pattern is what counts. Consider:

The happiness spreading with the practice—a happiness in knowing that some anonymous unknown brother might do for oneself what one is capable of doing, has done indeed, for other anonymous unknown brothers. And for countless others, who may have been, or may have been likely to be, victims of the unclean.

And conversely, consider the healthy fear in would-be trespassers everywhere. No more contempt for a mealy-mouthed, increasingly pusillanimous regular law. And (reverting to the general Victim-Public), as a consequence of such healthy fear, no more selling out to the *massively* unclean (in terms of government) in return for a more properly harsh set of laws. Everything done by isolated agents uncorrupted by formal organization. A real deterrent, because un-checkable, because myriad-headed.

Mere notes, of course. Mere fragments of a dream. Yet founded in fact. Good, solid, hard-won, practical experience. Thus one returns to the theory through practice. Thus one builds a body of increasingly valid and therefore fruitful theory. And then? More practice?

Hey, now, hold it, hold it right there!

One gets carried away.

No, though, really, one has to be truthful and confess that one feels quite firmly and definitely that one has dispensed with the practical for good. One is personally highly satisfied, fulfilled. One is all right, Jack.

But that says it.

One must never forget others. That way lies corruption. And that could engender problems, loss of power.

Even so: keep sense of proportion at all times.

His Journal:
Entry Number 10

Having read all that over in the full light of morning, I have to admit I was to a great extent playing with ideas.

After all, one has done enough in breaking the barrier, surely. One is happy (or, more correctly, in balance). One has achieved one's objective. Let others pick up the traces, take it from there.

Will try to find out more about those original Assassins, though.

Her Journal:
Entry Number 12

Oh what a lot I could write about that "golden period" he talks of. Oh how clear it all comes back, that wonderful May, that first week in June. Oh you have to believe him he must have felt good then whatever the crazy reasons he had. But no time. It's nearly four. He won't be much more than an hour now and this next bit is very important. Poor lamb if he really did think he'd done all that, if his silly game had got that far under his skin, just imagine the shock he got that second week in June when he first read the news, maybe in the very clipping he starts his next entry with.

I mean just read *this*.

And *imagine!*

TRAILER BLAZE SENSATION

OWNER ARRESTED

Aaron Schumaker, 60, of St. Louis, owner of the trailer in which five youths met their deaths from burning, last March, has been charged with the second-degree murder of Carl Schroeder, one of the dead youths.

Sheriff Willis R. Everett filed the charge in Municipal Court here today, saying that the move has been made "only after weeks of intensive undercover investigations in three states." Concerning the nature of the evidence, the sheriff stated that since March a great deal of information concerning Schumaker had been uncovered, including a 1958 charge in Illinois for importuning juvenile males. "This, together with the fact that we now have sworn evidence that Schumaker was seen the night previous to the murder deep in apparently friendly conversation with two of these boys, acted as a clincher. But there is more, much more, which we are not prepared to disclose at this time."

Schumaker, who appeared to be in a state of shock, collapsed shortly after the charge was filed and proceedings were adjourned sine die.

Outside the courtroom, colorfully clad Remington Le Strange, Jr., the attorney representing the interests of the families and friends of the deceased, who has recently come into nationwide prominence as the "Greasers' Lawyer," untypically refused to comment in detail. Asked if he was pleased at the development after protesting for months that the boys were completely innocent of the implied charge of arson, he said: "Sure I'm pleased. I'm always pleased on those occasions, so rare in this country these days, when justice overrides prejudice."

His Journal:
Entry Number 11

One can tell just by looking at him. One can tell just by glancing at his silly picture in the paper or on the screen. Glance indeed is all I can do, quickly, sideways, without letting the sick anger erupt.

"What's the matter, Ron, can't you bear to look at him?"

Trust Pat to notice something like *that*.

And that was all that was needed.

"What's the matter with the people in this country, you mean!" I snarled. "Can't they tell a phony when they see one by now? Jesus! Or is the bloody place so full of phonies they don't show up any more?"

"What, Ron? What is it? You've gone all white. You've—"

"No bloody wonder, is there? Just look at the smirking shit, just take a look! The public perhaps, but you wouldn't think the authorities would be taken in for one minute by that freakish—oh, what's the use?"

"You're beginning to sound like Gene Piscola. Just because he's got long hair and—"

"Gene Piscola my arse!"

"Well, don't shout, Ron, the neighbors will—"

"Sod the bloody neighbors. Most likely they're huddled over their televisions, lapping up that clown's every word anyway."

This is verbatim as near as I can make it.

Time: earlier this evening.

Subject: the television appearance of Mr. Remington Le Strange—

122

Mr. Remington very fucking Le Strange. Excuse me, but anyway that brings me to:

Reaction: fury, a white-hot impatient fury such as I never thought would ever engulf me.

"Can't you see, Pat," I said, trying to get a grip, "that that's just *it?*"

"What's just it?"

"His hair. It's phony too. You know me. *I* don't reach for my gun whenever—"

"You haven't got one, thank goodness!" (Laughing.)

"This is no laughing matter. This is a clear case of deliberate perversion of justice."

"What's his hair got to do with it, then? What's *he* got to do with it? He's only on the sidelines. And if that poor little man lost his temper that night, why blame—?"

"Oh, be quiet and listen a minute and you'll find out. What I'm saying is that it's not that lawyer bastard's long hair *as* long hair that I'm getting at, it's the fact that it's so false, it doesn't fit—"

"You think it's a wig?"

"It could be. But that's beside the point. Even if it's his own, most likely is, it's been grown for a purpose, *this* purpose, image bullshit. He's off now, thank God, but next time he comes on—and sure as hell he'll be seeing to it that there'll be many next times—you study the bastard's face, if you can stand it. Madison bloody Avenue. Shirt ad. He's as square as that turd of a sheriff in reality—"

"Ouch!"

"What's the matter?"

"Square turds!"

One had to smile. But only briefly.

"No, but you know what I mean."

And she stopped grinning and nodded and said yes, she thought she did, now that I'd mentioned it.

Oh, how I crave for equal time, for the chance to get on that screen right after the fucker and let all those millions see what I meant now that I mentioned it. Stupid, stupid bastards.

But of course anger and intemperate language don't help—beyond the safety-valve effect, now accomplished.

So, let us review the situation.

Schumaker has been, is being, framed. No doubt about that.

Shocked after the originating event, homeless—the trailer was now his home—he's been sweet-talked into staying available. One can just imagine the sheriff, concern written all over his big flat German pig-eyed face (maybe abetted by some bulky clucking hausfrau of his), saying: "Why don't you stay with your friends in Cambridge, Mr. Schumaker? Till you're feeling better. Don't you worry about money none, either. We got a slush fund here for contingencies like this. Right, John?" Nod from bleak-eyed thoughtful investigator at side, already sending out telex queries.

Or maybe *then*, right *then*, the concern was genuine, soured by only a touch of the normal routine precautions.

But then came the trouble.

Angry packs of greasers tearing around the countryside, thirsting for revenge. Threatening barns, farmhouses, farmers' daughters. Spontaneous enough at first, probably, but even then causing complaints, consternation, calls to the sheriff from Columbus: "Hi, Everett, any progress yet on the trailer affair? . . . Well now, this phone's been getting pretty hot. . . . Yeah, I know you boys are doing all you can, but we're getting reaction from the highway patrols and it is not complimentary, Everett. . . ." Or words to that effect.

Meanwhile, back on Madison Avenue, Smart-ass Le Strange takes a look in the mirror, decides it's long enough by now. In any case it will have to do, the time is ripe and ripeness is everything. Now where'd his secretary put those leathers? Ah yes. Too new-looking. "Thought I told you to drag them around the back stairs, Madge." "I really didn't have the heart, Mr. Le Strange, they're such good quality." "Oh, never mind. I'll get the janitor—hey, Oscar, you wanna make these look like they'd been well worn, man?" (Practicing the talk.) "Why, sure, baby" (taking advantage while the chance was there), "but how about I took 'em out onna the sidewalk an' eased some dogshit inna the seams?" "I'm not fooling, Oscar, and I don't have much time if I'm to catch that plane to Columbus." "And I ain't fooling neither, Mr. Lee Strange, sir. Because that's just what these Hell's Angels cats do, rub their gear in dogshit, stew it in piss. They also have to eat—" "Eating shit, Oscar, is a lawyer's specialty. Eating shit and shitting one-hundred-dollar bills. Now get with it, for Pete's sake!"

Thence to Ohio to strut around, talk to the greasers' friends, grease the reporters' palms, palm a few sly tricks. Hiring too no doubt some old reliable private snoop, digging, sick-visiting with Mr. Schumaker maybe, nothing put past that bastard. Snooping, grubbing, building his patient trap with mud and straw and butt ends, sniping at the sheriff in public but offering tidbits on the side as if unwillingly, letting them drop out, allowing himself to be bullied into handing them over. (*Was* there really anything in that 1958 charge? But even if there was, what the hell!) And suborning—certainly that—one would just like to see those local witnesses on the stand, that flabby local greasy-spoon proprietor, those two little gumchewing shits. But even so. A country that will be taken in by Mr. Le Strange shouldn't balk at even them, given a sufficiently skillful preliminary smear job.

Poor Schumaker.

His name doesn't help any. Outside New York.

And that sheriff. Willis may not be a German name, nor Everett, but by God he has the look of one.

But apart from that, only natural he should go along with the tide, the riding he must have been getting earlier. Suddenly seeing his way. Mr. Le Strange *and* Columbus off his back. Then, pathetically —oh, the big fat stupid pathetic hick-prick—adding his own little mite, the Everett Original:

"I always did have doubts when he said about the gas."

"Would you care to elaborate, sheriff?"

"Well, now, sure, why not? I guess it's been on record all along. Why get your emergency gas from a garage seven miles away when there's another only three miles down the road? Come to that, why not try the Birch farm, just a few hunret yards away? Knew to use their phone all right."

Elementary, my dear stupid Watson.

As if *that* fucking signifies.

But one waxes intemperate again. Cool it, Ron—as no doubt Mr. Le Strange would say.

It will come to nothing.

They'll have to drop the charge.

Poor Schumaker, nevertheless.

If there was anything one could *do*.

But no doubt he's enjoying it all, the limelight, meat and drink to them over here.

His Journal:
Entry Number 12

The picture gets gloomier, more ridiculous, week by week.

   Three samples:

1. *Piscola.* One might expect at least a certain disappointment here. One stops to check, passing by his yard the other afternoon, timing one's path to intersect that of the mower.

"What about those greasers *now*, Gene?"

"How's that?"

"The Ohio trailer affair."

"Oh. That. Yeah. Some turn-up, huh?"

"Taking back what you said about those kids, then?"

"Huh? Well, hell. It *could've* been them. How were we to know?"

"But now we know different, right?"

"Well, sure. The sheriff ought to—"

"Him and the longhair lawyer?"

"Argh! That shyster!"

Something in common, anyway.

"He seems to think these kids ought to be called Heaven's Angels."

"Yeah, well. It's his job. Guy's only doing what he's paid to. But I was reading an independent account about this Hell's Angels set-up. Some Army colonel, psychologist. Says they do have some good points."

"Jesus—"

"No. It made a lotta sense, Ron, I'd like you to read it. I'll get it out and—"

"Never mind. Just tell me in your own words, Gene. This I find very interesting."

"Well, sure. . . . I guess the main thing is the way these kids take care of their machines. Now *that* you don't hear about from your own kids when they're saying they admire these Hell's Angels and you're having to lift them by the lapels and tell them to mind their mouths. No. All you hear from them is about how great they look, and all that crap. But according to this unbiased article—and the guy's an Army colonel, remember—these kids keep their machines as clean and well tuned as the airlines keep their jets." He fondles the mower's parts—themselves slick, well kept—proud of their condition. "And I guess long hair or no, any kid looks after machinery the way it should be can't be all bad."

"But, Jesus, you're not telling me that prevents them from vandalizing other people's machinery?"

"Oh, I'm not saying they weren't messing around inside that trailer. What I am saying is that they had a reason. We know that now."

"You mean—"

"I mean it's open and shut. Now we know the details." He looks as if he could spit if it weren't that his immaculate mower might catch some of the spray. "Damned kike prevert!"

Heartfelt. So heartfelt that that is the way he pronounced it, quite unconsciously, him, an educated man (if you can call some of these Master's degrees they give away with candy wrappers tokens of an education).

Pre-vert!

Him! *Gene Piscola* speaking!

2. *Raybourn.* Standing at the station, Palmers Point, two mornings ago, waiting for train, dipping into *Times.* See a look of ineffable smugness cross fat face, see slitty eyes narrow further, green, cat with cream, if one can imagine pink-faced, close-shaved, after-shaved cat. Know without looking the item he's reading.

"Seems a lot more people agreeing with you now, Charlie," I say, by way of encouragement, speeding the test.

"Yes," he says, without looking up, so smugly sure of himself he doesn't bother to check the reference. "It was only elementary logic, after all."

"Yes, Mr. Holmes."

"Hmm?" Looks up now.

Wink.

"Forget it, Charlie."

"Well, damn it, what's so funny, Ron? You asked me. Nobody's saying I-told-you-so. All I'm saying is that it was my original logical option, before all the hoo-ha."

"So you're telling me."

"Look, what's eating you? What is it about this case that gets you so—"

"Your trouble, Charlie," gently laying a hand on his shoulder, "is you can't see any further than your pipe."

"Pipe?"

"Sorry. I was forgetting you don't smoke. Your nose, then. You can't see any further than your nose."

"Well, you tell me what I've overlooked."

"All I mean is that you're so hooked on this logic thing that if the real culprit stood in front of you, right where I'm standing now, and he said, 'Look, Charlie, I did it. I was there, Charlie. I was that missing witness that nobody seems to talk about any more. I was that so-called missing witness, Charlie, and I sent the little guy looking for a phone, and then I poured the gas in there, through the broken window with the bit of purple curtain clinging to it, next the door, deliberately next the door, how about *that*, Charlie?' Even then you'd stick to your original logical choice, wouldn't you?"

"Well, why not? I'd have to know something about that missing witness's motives before I'd buy *that* story. You bet."

He was looking at me sideways now. I was sweating, I noticed. But then the train came in.

Sometimes I wonder about Charlie Raybourn.

3. *The shoeshine boy.* I sought him out deliberately, this morning. I found I had an irresistible urge to see how it went with *him*. Only when I was seated did I realize I was wearing suede shoes, but no matter.

"Just shine around the edges of the soles and heels," I said.

"Your pleasure, mister," he said, shrugging. "But it'll cost you the same."

"Sure," I said, staring down at the paper, "sure. . . . Hey, how about this *now*?"

This time I was the one who tapped the item.

He glanced up. Thick curl of upper lip.

"Oh, *that?*"

"Yeah. Remember?" I said, remembering about the voice, clipping it, rasping it up. "Remember your theory?"

"About the missing witness?" No hesitation. "Yes indeedy. And you know something, mister? I'm still sticking to it. Those cops should be off their asses and looking for him still, right now. Yes sir! The Boston Burner."

"But you don't think they are. Right?"

"I do not think they are. *Right.* Why should they when they got a patsy all lined up already? Now if that Boston guy had been *black,* that's something else again—hyeeh! hee!"

He just laughed wheezily after that.

I tipped him well.

A good man, staunch and true.

Well versed in the ways of injustice.

His Journal:
Entry Number 13

Bleaker and bleaker.

Schumaker tried to kill himself in the prison hospital yesterday. Found razor blade in washroom, concealed it, slashed wrists in bed after dark but couldn't go through with it. Yelled for help, kept crying out he was sorry.

Fair-minded warden on television at pains to state that the apology was either to God or prison authorities or both for essaying a suicide and causing extra work. But of course the damage done. Clear sign of guilt. Sorry for what he'd done already, his terrible crime.

Big switch by Mr. Le Strange. No gloating. Sweeping back hair as if deep in thought, in reality tidying image for piety to follow, has gall to reproach reporters for asking question he probably bribed them to ask.

"What happened last night was between a man and his Maker. It is no concern of mine, or, with respect, any of us. What is my concern, your concern, everybody's concern, is what happened that night in March between a man and those immolated boys, between a man and, in fact, the people of this country."

What can one do against such bastards?

An anonymous letter, confessing?

Who would believe it? They get them all the time, one understands. Even in this case there have probably been a few cranks writing in.

But an anonymous letter with significant details? Details revealing a sure inside knowledge of the affair?

What details, though?

If only one had foreseen this development. Then one might have snatched some piece of evidence from the flames, something that only someone on the spot could have had access to, and sent *that* with a letter.

But again, what?

A charred scrap of material, to be matched forensically? A piece of one of the bikes, sufficiently personalized to be identifiable? Just what could one have taken that would be absolutely conclusive proof that the writer had done this thing?

And anyway, who is to say it wouldn't be ignored, quietly lost? As our man at Grand Central has already stated: Why bother when they have a good enough patsy all lined up?

Anonymous confessions, then, are out.

Besides, there's just an outside chance that all this might be a trap, with little Mr. S. conniving.

Doubt it, though.

Poor little devil.

His Journal:
Entry Number 14

This is an outrage!

This fair, clear-skied, for once unhumid August day—a day so beautiful that Pat and I had intended to spend it picnicking at the Ward Pound Reservation—will go down, *must* go down, as the blackest in American legal history.

It has just been announced that Schumaker has confessed!

Jesus Christ Almighty!

His Journal:
Entry Number 15

But one might have expected it.

It is all too obvious what has been going on.

He was—well, *is*, but one cannot help reverting to the past tense now—a very sick man. Quite clearly he was already that by the time he attempted suicide, but even earlier, even before the incident that started the whole grisly process, he must have been undermined by the death of his wife. Even *they*, even Mr. Smart-ass Le Strange, have never tried to imply that he did not love her, was not wholly devoted to her, was not as broken-hearted as he has been protesting he was, in spite of the 1958 business. Indeed, they seem to have been only too willing to give credence to this plus in his favor.

And now one begins to see why.

They must have been working on him in relays, grinding him down, softening him into mush.

First, the grinding, the crushing.

Every scrap of his less salubrious past—that less salubrious past we all have and which can be fed into the machine at any time. Every minor offense, misdemeanor, lapse, to say nothing of every misunderstanding and false accusation, every five and six that gossiping neighbors might have manufactured by bringing two and two together—everything that state and private shit-beetles could sniff out and drag back to base.

"So how about *that*, Mr. Schumaker?"

"And how about *this*, Mr. Schumaker?"

"Aw, come on, Aaron, don't tell us you've forgotten *there?*"

Like that. No doubt in carefully planned phases. Respectful/ hostile—one. Nakedly threatening—two. Friendly/coaxing—three.

No doubt with his own lawyers in some measure complying. And who is to say they weren't, in that respect, doing their best under the circumstances?

So finally he succumbed. Copping a manslaughter plea. Diminished responsibility. The farce has still to be presented publicly but the scenario can be read right now.

"You say that you can't remember exactly what happened."

Neither question nor statement. More of a suggestion.

"Well, I can, in a way, but now I don't know if what I remember did really happen if you see—"

"Yes. Of course. You've had these attacks before, Aaron?"

"Yes, but—"

"And you were upset, naturally—who wouldn't be?—badly upset by what was happening to your trailer?"

"Yes. Oh sure. Very. Yes. My wife and I had been—"

"Quite so. Extremely upsetting in any circumstances, but in this particular case even more so. Yes. But, Aaron—granted you were so badly upset, and no one's going to challenge that for a second —how can you be sure that you didn't have another attack there and then?"

"But I'm telling you I'm *not* sure! I mean I think I did. I mean I must have. I mean—"

"You don't *fake* these attacks, these blackouts, these brainstorms, do you?"

"Hey now, see here, I'm telling you the truth here, I—"

"Sure you are, Aaron. You're just a little confused is all. Anyone would be. Because if—*since*—since the attacks are genuine, you must be one of the last to be able to say exactly what you do during one. You do see that, don't you?"

And so on. In circles. Circles of sweet talk with the occasional kink, the hint of sharpness, of tangents.

With our friendly neighborhood psychiatrists on hand, one for them and one for you, Aaron, but both in this case anxious to help you, please believe us, so if you'll just cooperate, hold nothing back . . .

Jesus.

134

His Journal:
Entry Number 16

Well, there's nothing to be done about it now. I have given the matter my closest attention for a week, testing every possibility, but even the best is too remote to bear examination for long.

So there it is.

Aaron Schumaker. Just another innocent victim in the battle between good and evil. Anyone's good; anyone's evil. It happens all the time, whatever the cause, which is why it does happen all the time. So many causes. So many battles. So many bystanders.

Like the innocent victims of terrorists bombs in Belfast or Tel Aviv, New York, Munich, London. Or the innocent victims of legitimate sanctioned civilized bombs in Dresden or Coventry or Vietnam. Or the innocent hostage held in a suburban basement in Montreal or Buenos Aires.

Somewhere, at this moment, some government leader (yesterday's terrorist) is saying:

"If we give in to them over this, other attempts will follow, the floodgates of extortion will open up, releasing unprecedented—blah-blah-blah."

And somewhere, at this moment, some terrorist plotter (tomorrow's government leader) is saying:

"If we're not prepared to risk taking innocent lives, regrettable though that may be, we'll *never* succeed. They'll use that squeamishness, they'll—blah-blah-blah."

So, alas, with Schumaker.

But one promises him this: his contribution will not be forgotten. The next experiment shall be dedicated to you, Aaron Schumaker. Nor is that a mere emotional outburst, a piece of maudlin romanticized indulgence. One means it quite coolly. One *intends* it.

For it is, after all, a simple scientific progression. Because of this unfortunate development—or, rather, *unforeseen* development, for nothing is really unfortunate that occurs in the perfection-orientated trial and error of scientific experiment—the balance, poised so sweetly and seemingly so surely, has been destroyed again and must therefore be restored again. So the experiment conducted in the hope of restoring the balance must inevitably take into account the shortcomings of its predecessor. Measures, then, must be evolved, precautions planned, checks built in, to make sure that another mishap of a similar kind does not arise. Exactly what those measures shall be has yet to be determined. Maybe something along the lines sketched out in one of the entries above: the retention of some physical evidence that, in conjunction with an anonymous confession, will be sufficient to prove the innocence of any future Schumaker.

One begins to toy with the idea that nothing could serve such a purpose better than the weapon itself.

However . . .

Thus, in the sense outlined, without any formal declaration, the next experiment must inevitably and intrinsically be Aaron Schumaker's. Not Experiment Number Three but The Aaron Schumaker Memorial Experiment. As they do with lectures.

Already one begins to feel better.

So . . .

Back, as they say (but not with any sense of failure, rather with an eagerness to eradicate yet one more complex of flaws, one more colony of bugs, one more source of impurity), to the drawing board.

FOOTNOTE

Sustaining one in all this, a little positive in a blizzard of negatives, has been the discovery of a *sensible* account of the original Assassin Cult. Here is what the author has to say about the socio-religious aspect:

Her Journal:
Entry Number 13

But that can wait, it can be checked later if anyone's interested, I
know the book he got it from, because right now it is 5:35 and he
could be back any minute. I'm actually down in the basement, right
next to the toolbox, all set the minute I hear him drive—hey up, I
think he's

Her Journal:
Entry Number 14

Well get *me!*

After all that, after all those palpitations, after breaking a nail in such a hurry to snap that damned lock back on and nearly breaking my neck running up the basement stairs, who should it be but Jerry Grady, driving up *their* driveway and not Ron at all, not ours at all.

And then if that wasn't enough to make an honest woman curse, what happens five minutes after I've put the phone back on the hook and started to make a cup of tea (funny how you still fly back to it, times like these) if Ron doesn't call, snotty as you please, sure sign of being mad as hell.

"Well it's nice to know you've been spending a pleasant afternoon, anyway."

"Oh, Ron! Where are you calling from?"

"Where have I *been* calling from, for these past three hours, on and off? That's what you should be asking. Has something gone wrong?"

"Oh—that—oh—well it's been just one call after another. First May Zetlinger, you know what she's like, then—"

"Spare me the résumé, please. This is a toll call."

"Oh—yes—where did you say—?"

"I didn't. I will now. I'm up in Portland. Portland, Maine. It was going to be my last visit and I was all set to drive down this afternoon, but something's cropped up."

"Oh dear, no trouble—?"

"No, of course no trouble. It's just that I've been presented with the chance"—that's how he talks when he's mad and it's on the phone—"of clinching a very important deal."

"Oh, well that's good then?"

"Of course it's good!" Then I could hear a smile come into his voice, I'll say that, he never keeps the snot up for long—ugh, yik—what am I saying, but you know what I mean. "How are you, Pat?"

"Oh, fine. Great. When did you say—?"

"I didn't. Give me a *chance*. O.K.?"

"I'm sorry."

"Kiss?"

"Pchch!"

"That's better. Well look, it should be all settled this evening, over a drink. So all being well I'll be able to make a fairly early start to-morrow and be with you sometime in the middle of the afternoon. O.K.?"

So there it is.

Well.

Well at least I got everything down that matters, there aren't any more entries after that Assassin bit and I still don't think I'll bother with that. Well anyway, stupid, how can you with the notebook back in the box and the lock back on? Well I can always get the book he copied it from if it's still— But no. Waste of time anyway. No. No, the best thing now is to take it easy, Pat, just read what you've copied already all over before he comes and maybe fill in a few details from your side, about this past six months or so, since that time in May. Yes that's what I'll do.

And try and get an early night, you're looking quite haggard.

Yes, mother.

But right now I'm going to catch up on my eating never mind my sleep.

I wonder if he really does have a deal, though.

He sounded—

Oh don't be daft, Pat, of course he sounded strange, not being able to get you all those hours, anybody would.

Yes but I've suddenly remembered that Cleveland entry, that Experiment One, when he said he'd call me to say he'd been held up on business then, and he *has* been very edgy ever since that Schumaker thing, and—

Eat, girl. You're getting light-headed. You need some ballast.

Yes, mother.

Her Journal:
Entry Number 15

I wonder if he has something wrong with his brain or his glands, I mean all this talk about balance and juices and that, that keeps changing, making him walk on air one time and down in the dumps the next?

You hear of these cases all the time, just something mechanical, well *physical* really, but if you've got it whatever it is you yourself you don't know what it is, so you have to look around to account for it, to blame someone or something, or to be glad of something outside you, to make it fit. Am I making sense, doctor?

I mean somewhere I read something about it. Some old magazine. And what I'm getting at is this, is this all that's wrong with Ron?

"*All!*" she says.

But yes it's terrible but sometimes it only takes a little thing, like a little minor head operation, or even a drug like Mrs. Yeats next door to us back home with the thyroids.

Yes.

The more I

Phone.

Her Journal:
Entry Number 16

Well that was his lordship.

Deal can't be clinched till noon tomorrow for some reason, but that's definite and he'll certainly be leaving for home around that time so it will be evening tomorrow and not afternoon, so now you can take your time girl and get that early night. Nearly nine already and you are tired, the minute he said it and you knew the pressure was off, woomp she slumped.

Sounded quite chirpy. Maybe he'd been having one or two. But genuine enough, I mean if it had been a woman his first call would have covered it, because he's going to be up there all night anyway. And anyway, I don't think that's his trouble, my God I sometimes wish it was, was only that. Oh never mind.

Her Journal:
Entry Number 17

I've been reading it over what I wrote last night, before he called, and you know what? I really think I hit on something there, dog-tired or not. In fact maybe being so tired helped, helped me get right through to what really matters, oh I don't know.

Anyway. Where were we? Yes. This business of latching on to something outside to account for what's happening inside.

Well, the facts speak for themselves, don't they?

I mean going back to March. Yes. *That* was a real walking-on-air period and no mistake. All that irritability, it was like the snow, it seemed to melt after the Ohio trip and the trunkful of flowers. I mean the facts.

That was when he started wearing silk pajamas, remember?

"My skin feels all seething, especially at night, so no more cracks about catching something from Gene Piscola, you hear?" (Joking about it, full of cracks again.) "No, but truly, Pat, I feel I need something more sympathetic against the skin to keep it from seething at night. Days, I don't mind it. It's very stimulating, like wearing after-shave all over. But one does need one's sleep."

And *that* was when he started showering more often, twice a day at least, more when he was at home, I mean as well as his regular old British boiling-hot tub last thing at nights.

And *that* (yes, because you did begin to wonder about a woman again, even though not seriously) was when he started getting his nails manicured regularly, something he used to sneer at when he

142

first came over, saying, "Some of these New York types are proper poofters!"

And *that* was when he became more American all of a sudden in other things, but mainly his accent. Sometimes in the early days over here, especially that sticky six months in the first spring and summer he used to criticize me, quite snappish sometimes, saying:

"Oh well—now Pat—she changed her accent on the plane coming over."

"Well what if I did?" I used to snap back. "When in Rome do as the Romans do is what I say."

Then sometimes, if he wasn't in too snappish a mood, he'd grin and say:

"So long as you don't do *everything* the bastards do!"

And then I'd know he was sorry for passing the remark.

Yes.

May in particular was a high spot. My new all-American Ron I used to call him and he'd laugh and take it all in good part. And that was probably because as he says in those horrid reports he'd been more settled in his happiness. I mean late March and April his happiness was a bit creepy, like he said his skin felt, something not quite natural about it, but May was lovely, settled, deep-down happiness. Naturally I was a tinchy bit disappointed about his change of attitude about moving from P.R.P. to N.Y.C., and I guess I must have let it show, as he says. But not when he explained, I wasn't a bit disappointed then and I had to agree that things were so different this May that Palmers Point might have been another place altogether. I mean not only the dogwood itself, but people's faces here when they looked at you they had that open, bright, friendly look of the dogwood flowers themselves. If you see what I mean.

Mind you—

No—

Maybe—

Well, yes, better keep the record as full as possible, Mrs. Bracknell, we never know what might be valuable, well all right then. There *was* just a little cloud.

It was while we were discussing the New York move, that's what has reminded me, and I said something, now let me get it exactly. Yes. I said:

"Well one drawback to a New York apartment, even if you are in town all the time, will be storage. I was only thinking yesterday, I don't know what we'd do without a basement."

He suddenly went all still and sharp.

"Basement? Storage? What d'you mean?"

"Basement," I said. "Come on, Ron, you're all-American now. It's what we say instead of cellar. And storage, that's a word that means—"

But he was laughing again by now. Cloud gone. And he said:

"I'll be storing something in your basement, baby, if you don't cut it out!"

And then—but that's our business.

The point is of course that now I can see why he should be a bit touchy about the basement, even in his happy periods, with the book right there in the toolbox, and that's why he was so sharp in picking me up. But naturally not knowing about the book then, I had meant it innocently enough and he must have been able to see that, and so the cloud passed away. His brain or his glands were still set for Happy.

But then that second week in June.

Oh my God.

This little lever in his brain must have gone click like a time switch or that little bit of iodine in his glands must have fallen below the correct level. (People should have little green windows like in that old dishwasher we once had to say when the chemicals should be topped up.)

Anyway, click, and there was the Schumaker arrest, readymade, nothing to him really, but very annoying to find Charlie Raybourn had been right again and himself wrong.

And so the snapping again. And letting himself go, I mean in the bad sense, no more manicuring, cutting down the showers even though it was getting hotter, things like that. And more than anything seeming hungrier and hungrier for the *bad* news, reading everything he could lay his hands on about the Schumaker business, crouching over the TV, just *asking* to be annoyed, to feel let down, to feel betrayed, well *wronged* then, badly wronged, like Dad after the War, with the Labour Government. I was only little then but I knew to duck whenever Attlee, Bevin, any of them were mentioned on the radio, especially Cripps, well so it was with Ron and this Schumaker business and it wasn't even politics, I ask you! Frothing at the mouth nearly, just like Dad, simply *letting* it get under his skin.

And another thing it reminded me of whenever that Greasers' Lawyer was on the TV, I could swear Ron's teeth chattered just like that old cat we once had when it saw sparrows fluttering outside the window, and he was a tom too. Why *are* men like that about stuff that doesn't really concern them, as if they *like* getting mad, as if they've simply got to have *something* to get mad about?

Anyway, honestly, I got to feeling all tight whenever he looked at the paper or switched on the news, bracing myself, and when Schumaker tried to commit suicide you'd have thought it was the end of the world, striding about and smacking his hand with his fist. He even went back to wearing ordinary shorts for a spell, and snapping like a bad-tempered dog—at me, his friends, anyone and everyone, his clients too, I shouldn't wonder. And then came the comments, what everybody was thinking the suicide attempt proved.

My God.

Not any snappier, he couldn't get any worse in that direction. In fact if anything I think he went quieter, which was worse, because it was a sick grim deadly sort of quiet at times, believe me, and all at once he stopped being all-American, and became more British again, much more, his accent especially, and he even mentioned once or twice about going back to England, something he'd never done before, especially on the vacation in Bermuda, but not *because of* the English there, *in spite of* them, what a vacation. If he wasn't puking at the English there he was spitting blood about the Americans, and all the time wanting the next newscast to hurry up or the next edition of the papers. Thank God it was only one week out of the two.

And then the confession. Just after we got back. Second week of vacation.

Beautiful day, like he said. All set for a picnic, like he said. Seemed quieter that day, glad to be home even if it was only Palmers Point.

Then this news.

I tried to reason with him.

"But he's *confessed*, Ron. People don't confess to something they haven't done."

"Don't they?"

Quiet. Looking up from where he was sitting, hunched, crouched. Flash of teeth, like a soft snarl. But damn it I'm his wife and *someone* had got to try and reason with him.

"No, of course not. Not in a free country. This isn't a dictatorship, after all."

"Isn't it?"

Same look, same flash of teeth.

"Well you know it isn't!" I said, getting mad myself.

But of course, dictatorship or not, people do confess to things they haven't done. I know that now. Look at all this he's written himself. He must have had that at the back of his mind when we were arguing. Because of course he *hasn't* done any of these things, not really, not he, not Ron, my Ron.

Yet even so, as I said before and I'll say it again, this doesn't mean that we've got to laugh it off—*laugh!* some *laugh!*—certainly not. Making all this up, these details, it's enough to give you the creeps, and something will have to be done, that's for sure. If a doctor was to read that notebook he'd soon tell you that, my girl. Your husband is a very sick man, Mrs. Bracknell, and the sooner he gets treatment—

Oh well.

Well.

Let us see. Let us just see when he comes back this evening. Let us just study him carefully this next day or two, in the light of all this—"light" she says!—in the *dark* of all this, more like, in the *shadow* of all this—yea though I walk in the valley of—now now, chin up, Pat, nothing's ever as bad as it seems—and then maybe if he's still snappy and irritable get him to see the doctor, just in the ordinary way, just a check-up, but give the doctor a bit of warning, a hint, that should be enough at first, no need to show him all this at first, and then play it by ear from there.

He'll thank you for it in the end, Pat. Sure he will, it's your duty, girl, in sickness and in health, remember?

But be careful. Now you have seen the book it wouldn't do to let him get the least little bit suspicious again, like that time in May, because this time the cloud wouldn't be so little and it would be a whole lot blacker and there's no telling what might happen if it suddenly burst.

Anyway.

Am I too late to book a hair appointment, I wonder?

Her Journal:
Entry Number 18

Well *something's* happened.

The lever has clicked to Happy again all right.

And how!

You'd have thought he'd been away for years, like coming back from a war or something, tooting the horn all the way up the driveway, storming in, bunch of chrysanthemums in one hand, bottle of champagne in the other already iced, kissing me, lifting me up, swinging me around, mussing my hairdo, and switching me over onto the couch and—well, that's our business again although it was nearly every single damned one of our neighbors' business as well, and would have been for all he cared, if I hadn't made him stop a minute and give me time to switch out the light and pull the drapes.

But although I was laughing and I was happy too, there was something, well, *several* things.

One, it was the seething jumpy kind of Happy state again. Obviously.

Two, it really was as if he'd been in a war because he'd got these two deep long nasty-looking scratches on his face, his left cheek.

And three, his coat, the gabardine London Fog thing that he'd never have bought in England, but which he'd bought during his all-American period. It was still damp, as if it had been soaking wet, and all creased where he'd stuffed it anyhow in a corner of the back seat. That's not like my neat Ron at all, in any of his moods. His pants bottoms were in a state too, creases all gone, and his shoes, you know how they get when they've really had a soaking, all that white marbling, powdery, like salt.

Number Two was what concerned me most of all though.

"My God, what have—?" I began to say, as soon as he came in, but that's when the kissing and the hugging and lifting and swinging started and I couldn't get another word in edgewise for quite a long time after that.

But when I could and we were sipping the champagne, I did, and he just shrugged and said:

"Oh, it's nothing."

"But it looks as if you've been *clawed*, Ron."

"Well so I have."

"Well go on then, don't just sit grinning. Who by?"

"A tiger, what else?"

"No, come on, Ron, seriously. It looks as if it might need treatment. What did it?"

"A piece of outdated machinery," he said.

"You haven't been in a car crash or—?"

"No. Not that kind. Packaging equipment. At least it wasn't rusty. Not *that* old."

"Pack—?"

"The place in Portland I was at this morning. I was demonstrating our latest sealing machine, and to compare it I switched on one of the contraptions they were still struggling along with."

"Well?"

"Well the bloody thing went haywire. Just broke up in our faces. Luckily I was the only one hurt."

"Luckily! It looks as if it could have taken your eye out!"

"Well it didn't, love, did it?"

He seemed just a little bit needly, so I waited till he'd had another sip.

"You could sue them, couldn't you?"

"Sure. But not when it happened to double-clinch a fifty-thousand-dollar contract. They couldn't sign it quick enough after that. . . . Now what's to eat? I'm starving."

That was last night.

This morning he's busy in his den upstairs. Writing out his reports, he says.

He means his business reports, of course.

But I think I know different now, because you see he went down into the basement first, and I heard him opening the toolbox, and I think we can be pretty sure it wasn't to get a spanner or a refill for his pen. I mean right up until this last few days I had never given his report-writing sessions a second thought, but I bet if I had I would have noticed the routine was always the same, or nearly always, with the trip into the basement coming first. In fact now that I think about it I can remember some of the excuses—sometimes, like today's, to check on the furnace, but more often to look for an old catalogue or price list in the pile under the workbench—and every time a visit to the toolbox as well I bet, you old slyboots, Ron.

If only I had a duplicate key!

Her Journal:
  ## Entry Number 19

It's no use. I had to do it. I couldn't sleep last night for thinking about it.

So as soon as Ron set out for the station this morning I called Mr. Jones.

He wasn't in. His wife said could she help and I asked where he'd be and she told me, a new house being built the other side of town. I waited until I could be sure the New York train would have gone, just in case Ron called from the station about something, not that he ever does, but now you just can't be too careful, Pat my girl, and then I went to seek out Mr. Jones.

He looked a bit surprised but I'd got my tale ready.

"Mr. Jones," I said, "you remember borrowing that spanner, that wrench of my husband's when you so kindly fixed the tap, I mean faucet?"

"Yup!" he said, speaking a bit quicker than usual. "And I remember giving it back to you. Into your own hand. Yes, ma'am. I remember I wiped it dry and—"

"Yes, Mr. Jones. Of course. So do I. It's not that. It's just that I did a very silly thing."

"Oh?"

"Yes. When you used that key and opened the box and I took out the wrench and you went up the stairs with it, you know what—?"

"Hee, hee! Don't tell me, ma'am. You went and snapped the lock back on, right?"

"Right," I said. "And—"

"No, don't tell me!" This was making his day. I was only hoping he wouldn't make a day of *it*. "When you came to replace the wrench I'd already gone, right?"

"Right."

"But being a lady you kind of didn't let it bother you none, knowing your man wouldn't be back for a few days, right?"

"Right again, Mr. Jones."

"But come the weekend and he got back, suddenly you remembered it, right? And then you was hoping and praying he wouldn't go near that box, least not to get him the wrench, right?"

"Mr. Jones, you ought to be a thought-reader. Right, right, right. So—"

"So now you've come to Jonesy to ask if you can borrow that key again, right?"

I just nodded, smiling, being careful to keep an admiring shine in my eyes and the impatient gleam out.

"Well now," he was already bending over his box, lifting the great bunch of keys, "I just don't have the time right now to stop by—"

"No, if I could just borrow it, Mr. Jones. I'll bring it back right away."

He grinned.

"Take your pick," he said.

I gaped. "But—"

"My fun," he said. "Naw. I know my keys. It was either—" he tugged one loose—"this'n, or—" he tugged another loose—"this'n."

I put out my hand, hoping he was right.

"Ah-ah!" he said. "The rental's twenty bucks a key!"

I gaped again, but you know, I think I'd have been prepared to pay that, I was so desperate. Then he broke up, wheezing and laughing.

"I do believe you think I mean it. Old Jonesy, who never overcharged by so much as a nickel the whole of his life. Here, ma'am, my pleasure."

He was chuckling all the time it took me to get back to the car.

"I'll bring them back right away," I said.

He waved the offer aside.

"Any time," he said. "Whenever you're passing."

So here I am, with the book in front of me once more and all the day to read and copy Ron's latest bit of nonsense in, yet somehow, oh I don't know, but now I have it I just don't feel like opening it at all, I feel—well—oh well, press on, Pat, it's your duty, girl.

Her Journal:
Entry Number 20

Great merciful God in heaven above!
  No wonder I was so reluctant to start in reading it!
  No wonder I can hardly hold the pencil!
  I've just finished reading his latest entry and honestly
  Well.
  Just listen, read *this!*

His Journal:
Entry Number 17

It wasn't meant to turn out like this. But then so many of the great seminal experiments of science history were like that. One thinks of Pasteur, seeking a method of preventing beer and wine from going "off," only to discover the principle of immunization. Or something of the sort.

At all events, this has turned out better, exactly right. While fulfilling all the conditions of Bracknell's Law as originally envisaged—anonymity, randomness, cleansing action, etc.—and incorporating the later principle of optimum opportunity, it also embodies (one intends no pun!) the modifications found to be necessary after the Schumaker fiasco.

Once again, one notes the role of opportunity, this time more pronounced in importance than ever. Indeed, one had not even intended buying the gun up there, let alone conducting the experiment. All one had decided was to use the instrument for this—very crucial—experiment: a handgun, no footling about with shotguns requiring possibly difficult, certainly skillful sawing down to size. No. Something simple was required, something sure, safe to handle, easily concealed. But it was in New York or some other really big city that one was planning to obtain it, after the necessary research, the necessary reconnaissance of likely bars.

Yet on Thursday evening opportunity arrived in a bar in which one had no thoughts of reconnoitering, simply a quiet if some-what sleazy place in which to mull over one's plans regarding the form the experiment should take. In fact, at the moment of contact it was purely business that was occupying my mind: merely the sort of contemplation of the following day's negotiations indulged in by any representative.

"Nothing much doing here in winter."

Thus, with a heavy sigh, Opportunity took its seat at the bar, next but one to mine.

I was annoyed at first. The place was practically deserted, and I was annoyed that this tall gray-faced stranger with the lean flabby jowls, the snub nose, the yellow-gray hair dressed d.a. fashion twenty years out of date, should choose to sit by me, disturbing the line of thought and spoiling my drink with the reek of his cheap deodorant.

"I wouldn't know," I said, hoping to indicate (a) that one was a transient, and (b) that one wasn't interested.

He didn't seem to care what I wished to indicate.

The bartender was at the far end, talking to a man in a merchant sailor's uniform, but I noticed that the intruder already had his drink, a lager it looked like. Clearly, he had approached from one of the tables behind, having deliberately picked me out, despite his simulation of casualness.

"Course," he said, addressing the rows of bottles on the shelves in front of him rather than me, "if you know the right places, any city, any time of the year—heh!—any time of the *day* . . ."

"Yeah." I adopted a bored, clipped, not-interested tone. I adjusted the accent too, exaggerating the Americanness. If I let him know I was British I'd have to hear all about his pre-D-day experiences in England. He was that age. Probably Navy. Not unlikely dishonorably discharged from the Navy. Clear blue eyes—but shifty. Shifty—but sardonic. I could see them clearly now, flicking to and from mine in the reflection between the Jack Daniel's and the Old Forester bottles. "Dare say you could."

Again the completely non-interested tone. Fuck off, in short, to be frankly exact.

"You're a stranger in these parts . . . ?"

Barely a question. More a probe, as if playing a quiz game.

I sighed heavily. You're on my back, buster. Fuck off.

"Yeah."

Misinterpreted again. Deliberately, or just dumb?

"First time in Portland?"

"Second."

I could have bitten off my tongue. Its passion for exactitude is always leading me into false positions.

"Business, I reckon."

He said it with such disappointment in his voice, a certain resignation, that I was encouraged to speed him on his way.

"You could say that."

That seemed to do the trick. He sipped his lager, looked at his watch, hummed a snatch of a tune, glanced around. Obviously waiting for someone, just killing time, any moment now he'd shove off, no further problem.

Then suddenly he turned, put a hand on my sleeve, fixed his eyes on my necktie, and said, in a much lower voice than he'd used up until now:

"If you'd like to switch to a joint with more action, girls, know what I mean—?"

His hand was huge, but long rather than broad. Yellow, sinewy, hairy, with black-edged nails. I stared at it. He took it off quickly.

"Not interested."

He shrugged.

"Suit yourself. I only thought . . ."

Muttering something I couldn't catch, he swung off the stool and went down the bar with his empty glass.

"Hey, Ed! How about a little service?"

He joined the bartender and the sailor in their conversation.

Even then I failed to recognize the opportunity. All I felt was glad to be rid of him. Then annoyed because he'd broken the train of my business thoughts. Then, into the vacuum there started drifting the deeper current of thoughts, the next experiment, the decision about the gun, the—

And then I began to wonder.

I studied him covertly. He was talking with his wide loose mouth, grinning, nudging the sailor, stabbing one of his black-clawed fingers at the bartender's chest, obviously an habitué, a tout of some kind if not a pimp, and just the sort of person one had prefigured as being of use.

I ordered another drink while I considered it.

Then another while I waited for him to glance my way.

He didn't. I almost left it at that. But then I saw him drain his glass, clap the sailor on the shoulder, and begin to move up the bar, on his way out.

I let him get past for a few steps (still he hadn't glanced at me again), then called:

"Hey!"

"Huh?"

"Maybe there is something you can do for me."

He leered, then came and sat by me again.

"What'll you have?" I said.

He ignored it.

"Changed your mind, huh?" he murmured. "What'll *you* have?"

I shook my head.

"No. Not a woman—"

"Ah, *well* now!" He leered again, tapping his nose with a finger three times as long. "Maybe—"

"And not a boy, either," I said, a bit annoyed again. Perhaps I should drop it altogether.

He shrugged.

"What other kinda hole *is* there, mister?"

Still leering. Then suddenly his face went serious, no doubt in tune with mine.

"Aw, Jesus!" he said. "Sorry. It's a *game* we're talking about, huh? *That* kinda action. Well now—no?"

Mr. Fixit all right. Instinct correct after all.

"No," I said. "I'd like to know—" I looked around and dropped my voice and he leaned forward, all ears and pine deodorant—"where I could buy a gun."

He sat up with a jerk. Then looked at me slowly, moving up from my necktie to my eyes—then swiftly back.

"A *piece?*"

"If that's what you want to call it, yes."

I felt more confident. He wasn't at all shocked, merely stalling, wondering where he could obtain the merchandise at such short notice, just another businessman.

"Without bothering about no license, I presoom?"

"Your presumption is correct. . . . You sure you won't have another drink?"

"Nuh-huh."

156

He waved the offer aside, his eyes almost shut, frowning, thinking, then darting a very doubtful look at me out of the corners.

"Well now, it all depends—"

"Oh, it's only for self-defense. You know. Traveling around. Something to know that you have in the glove compartment."

"Yeah?"

"Look, forget it."

He probably couldn't meet the order in time anyway.

"No. No." A flicker of anxiety, laced with obsequy. A businessman about to lose an order. "All I'm thinking of is it depends what kinda piece."

"Well, I obviously don't want an automatic rifle for the glove compartment."

"Yeah, yeah, but I was going to say—and how much you're willing to pay."

I shrugged. I hadn't really gotten around to thinking about this side.

"Oh—forty, fifty dollars."

He looked cautiously at my eyes, then his mouth spread in that slack leer again.

"You want a piece fires *real* slugs? I mean a *reliable* piece?"

"Sure."

"Well, it'll sure's hell cost you more than that, mister."

I wondered, but didn't say anything. He must have misinterpreted my silence. He was backing off a little but giving nothing away. A businessman all right, every readjusting inch of him.

"You see, there might be expenses. Might have to take a trip down to Portsmouth."

"Portsmouth?"

"Yeah, about forty miles south of here. Big naval base. I got friends there. And if you want a really *reliable* piece, where better?"

"So?"

"So like I said, there'll be expenses. Travelin' expenses. Outapocket expenses. Because while I'm taking a trip down there I can't be doing no hustling here, now can I? You willing to go up to seventy-five?"

"If it's worth it. And it doesn't take forever."

"How long you here for?"

"*Here?* In here?"

"Portland."

"Tomorrow."

"Be here tomorrow night and I'll let you know. Same time."

He said it with such finality and assurance that I knew he could swing it. It would mean staying another night, of course—or driving down through the night—but what the hell. With the gun safely purchased, one could give one's whole attention to the details of the conduct of the experiment.

I finished my drink, looking at him the whole time. I could feel the balance reasserting itself already, the assurance of Newstrander and the other five rising inside me. He must have seen something of it in my eyes. He looked most respectful.

"O.K.," I said. I tossed a ten-dollar bill on the counter. "That more than covers my tab," I said. "Get yourself another drink out of it. Be sure to."

He nodded. He knew what I meant. I didn't want him following me back to the motel, checking.

"Sure," he said. "I'll have a lager. See you tomorrow"—he leered one last time—"and not before."

He was a businessman.

There was a slight risk, obviously. In spite of all precautions, absolute anonymity couldn't be absolutely guaranteed. But it was a risk that could be nicely calculated. For one thing, there was no intention of using the gun in that neighborhood, and therefore no chance of the vendor's putting two and two together (or three and eight, or four and five) whenever the result of the experiment should be publicly announced. Once it had left his hands it would disappear with the purchaser into the teeming violent hinterland, where shootings were everyday occurrences—indeed, every-*hour* occurrences, one suspects, even every-*minute* occurrences. Nothing to connect that particular gun with any one of those.

So all that remained to worry about was would he in fact be able to deliver.

He was already waiting in the bar on Friday evening.

"Order first," he murmured out of the side of his mouth as I slipped onto a nearby stool. "Well, hello again!" he said in a loud voice, making a show of turning toward me. Then to the bartender: "Ed!"

He said nothing further as the bartender served me. The place was as quiet as the previous evening and for a moment I feared that Ed might hang around, wishing to make conversation. But either he was in a sullen mood or my man had already warned him off, because he went back to the far end of the bar and began poring over a newspaper.

"Well?" I said.

"You're in luck, mister."

"Good."

"But it's gonna cost you ninety."

I can't say I was surprised. I shrugged.

"We'll see. Where is it?"

He pretended to gag over his sip of lager. Then wiped his mouth with the back of one of those black-clawed hands.

"You don't think I brung it *here*, do you? Middle of a busy district like *this?*"

"Well, where—?"

"Tomorrow, mister."

"But you said—"

"Sorry. But it has to be tomorrow."

"Tomorrow morning I'll be leaving. Looks like I've been wasting too much time already."

"Tomorrow morning's when I *mean*. That's when I pick up the gun. It's all arranged."

"You mean—"

"Like I said. I got friends in Portsmouth. You want a service thirty-eight, good as new, or don't you?"

"Sure, but—"

"So tomorrow, early, I pick it up, place near Portsmouth, just this side, then I bring it up this way, place near Portland, just *that* side. Got it? I mean you don't *really* expect me to deliver right here in town, do you?"

I had to admire his own precautionary instincts.

"How early?"

"Well now, that ain't strictly within my control. Depends on the other guy, any snags his end. Best make it late morning, be on the safe side. Noon suit you?"

"Fair enough. Where? What place?"

"You know the area well?"

I shook my head.

"Well, it's pretty easy. Listen . . ."

He gave me the name of a beach area a few miles south, with precise routing directions.

"When you get there, you'll see a place where they sell snacks in summer, with a parking lot. Nice and private. Be there at noon and we'll close the deal then."

It sounded a bit off-track, even granting the need for precautions.

"Couldn't we just make it someplace on the turnpike, a service area? It shouldn't be too difficult to find a quiet corner of the parking lot there."

His mouth twitched in a contemptuous grin.

"Turnpike! Jesus—"

"All right, someplace on Route One then!"

"Mister!" He laid a claw on my sleeve again, quickly, gently, then took it off as quickly. "You're no sucker, right?"

"Right!"

"Sure. I never thought you was. So you'll be wanting to examine the merchandise, right? Maybe fire off a coupla rounds. You figuring on taking potshots at a passing highway patrol by way of a tryout?"

I had to grin.

I finished my drink.

"Noon tomorrow then." I stood up.

Again the claw on my sleeve.

"Ain't you forgetting something?"

"Am I?"

"A little something on account? Make sure I don't have a wasted morning?"

I'd thought of this.

I took out two twenties.

"Forty enough to convince you?"

His eyes flickered greedily. Already his hand was out below the counter.

"Sure. Yeah."

"Right." Keeping my own hands down, I ripped the bills in half. "The other two halves tomorrow and another fifty to go with them. O.K.?"

He gave me a grudging leer.

"You sure *are* some businessman, ain't you?" he said, echoing back my own thoughts of last evening.

"Be sure to finish your drink," I said, giving him a cheerful wink but taking care to keep my smile cold.

I saw what he meant about privacy as I drove past the empty ticket booth at the entrance to the park. The rain was beating down and the only sign of life was the occasional seagull, wheeling and dipping and being tossed about by the wind. Even if it had been a fine day, I don't suppose there would have been many people around, this time of the year, because, as he'd been at pains to point out, this was strictly a bathing spot, with no fishing or anything like that.

The pavement twisted gently between low mounds of grayish grassland, leading toward swaying trees, evergreens of some sort, and a low white building, beyond which the ocean writhed angrily, moodily. The parking lot itself was unavoidable, giving one no chance for the circumspection one suddenly felt was required. A bend in the pavement around a somewhat higher knoll and suddenly it was there, wet black reflecting white, with the only other car, a battered old Chevvy that just had to be his, parked in the far corner.

I hesitated.

Suddenly, as I say, I had begun to wish it wasn't *so* private out here. Suppose it was a trap?

But then I smiled and drove on, drawing alongside.

"Hi!" The leer greeted me as I wound down the window. "Find it O.K.?"

I looked at my watch.

"It's still before noon, isn't it? Yeah. Sure. I got the clerk at the motel to go over the directions you gave me. Just to be on the safe side."

His leer broadened. He cocked his head on one side and slid his eyes appreciatively.

"You told him you was coming here, huh? But I bet you didn't say what for!"

We were still in our respective cars. Talking across through the open windows.

"No. I told him I'd met a guy in a bar who'd promised to show me some good fishing. I even told him which bar, and what the guy looked like. I did that when he said he'd never heard there was fishing here. I said well this guy looked like he knew what he was talking about, a real colorful local character I said, and he said well it could be so then."

He was laughing. Not because he could tell I was lying but rather because he believed me, because it was just the sort of precaution the two torn bills might have led him to expect.

"Argh, c'mon!" he said, getting out. "We're wasting time." And, as I was slow to move even then: "Here." He held out a bundle, rather bigger than I'd expected, wrapped in what looked like a piece of dark plastic raincoat. "You hold on to it if it makes you feel easier."

I unwound the plastic far enough for me to see that it was indeed a gun: a slick well-oiled revolver with a heavy butt and a longish barrel, maybe over-long to be ideal, but looking good anyway, and feeling even better.

"Come *on*," he said. "It's kinda cold standing here. You wanna try it out or not?"

I stuffed the gun into my raincoat pocket, after wrapping it loosely again, and got out. It *was* cold and the wind was stronger than I had imagined it. Beyond the deserted building a flagpole was rattling, and beyond that came the snapping and booming of the waves. They sounded like guns themselves. Big guns. A few practice revolver shots would be completely lost out there.

"You picked a good spot," I yelled, as we turned the corner of the building into the full blast of the wind.

"Yeah!"

He plucked my sleeve. He looked top-heavy in the thick short peajacket, but more than ever like an ex-sailor as he rolled with the gusts.

"Over here, I thought," he said.

He led me past the trees and wet forlorn picnic tables. One of these was overturned, reminding me of something I couldn't put a name to right then: something emotionally vivid but pictorially vague. I remember *now*, of course.

Anyway, we stepped carefully through the stringy wind-bent grass and down a ledge or shelf onto the beach. The sand was too wet to be blown about, but even so the wind was strong enough to make its color change even as one looked, lightening momentarily before the rain and spray turned it dark again.

He plucked my sleeve once more, drawing me toward some rocks, nearer the sea. Some were quite big. The ground became rougher, rocky itself, slippery in parts. Seagulls' screams pierced the lulls between blasts. Their screams and the artillery noises the waves were making.

We crouched in the lee of one of the larger rocks.

"O.K.," he said, his blue eyes ranging back and forward inland, "this should be good enough. Wanna try her now?"

I nodded, pulling out the wrapped gun.

"It's O.K.," he said, noticing my hesitation. "Jeez! A little rain ain't gonna hurt *that* piece. Here, let me."

I gave him the bundle, no longer doubting his intentions. He unwound it gently, almost with pride.

"Beauty, ain't she?"

"Yes," I said, meaning it.

Suddenly it leaped in his great claw.

"Stick 'em up!" he snapped.

I gasped. I must have looked completely astounded.

He laughed.

"Heh! heh! My fun, mister. Couldn't resist. But hey—come *on*— whaddya take me for? Besides, she ain't loaded. See?"

He snapped it open.

"Look," I said, feeling the sweat trickle down my ribs despite the wind, "let's cut the shit and get down to—"

"Which brings me to another slight point," he said, yelling against a particularly strong blast above our heads, over the rock. "We didn't mention anything about shells. With these it's gonna come to ninety-five. That O.K.?"

"These" was a cardboard carton. He handed me the gun while he removed the lid and plucked out the bullets with his black nails, almost daintily.

"O.K.?"

"O.K.," I said nervously.

But it was an affected nervousness.

For even as he removed the lid and I felt the firm butt in my hand, inspiration had come. It had come on the wings of the wind, fierce and penetrating, screaming like a gull, heralded by a multi-gunned salute from the tossing restive ocean. It had come with another memory, a boyhood memory, of an old movie, a Cagney movie, in which *he* had affected nervousness when purchasing a gun.

Why not?

Here and now?

A creep like this—a pimp, no doubt a bully, maybe even a killer himself when he felt he could get away with it, a roller of drunken seamen certainly if not one of your actual muggers, modern style. Such an opportunity might not come your way for a long, long time.

And the poetry of it.

The economy. Beautiful.

Schumaker, I thought, just cross your fingers.

"Er"—with a nervous dicker as he began to load—"you sure . . . it . . . there's no danger—"

Another blast overhead.

"What?"

"You sure there's no danger?"

"Danger?"

"I mean—they're the right size, huh?"

"*Sure* they are!" He pushed the last one home. "Take a look."

"I mean—well—you hear about guns blowing up in the user's face."

He grinned. This was making him feel good.

"Argh, come on!" He moved around the rock, facing the sea. "I'll fire the first myself."

He did. Twice. Into the wet sand about ten yards ahead. Two furrows, deep, short, suddenly appeared.

"O.K.?"

"O.K."

"You wanna—?"

"No. No. That's O.K."

He grinned, motioning me back around to the lee again.

"You brung the money?"

"Sure. Here." I pulled out the tight wad that I'd got all ready. "The two half-twenties and sixty more, also in twenties. I'll need change. And the gun."

He looked, then laughed, holding it out by the trigger guard.

"You *are* an ugly one, mister, no mistake. . . . Thanks."

He took the wad as I took the gun.

He began counting, hunched over the wad, taking care not to let the wind snatch it from him. I looked around. Only the gulls.

"I'm not sure I do have the change," he began, "but—"

That's when I pulled the trigger.

He jerked back, as if blown against the rock by a wind even stronger than the one overhead, his hands still clutching the wad, his eyes wide.

"Why—" he cried.

His clutch loosened.

Blood was already spilling out from his chest, onto his hands, presumably onto the bills also.

He let them go.

They fell, then fluttered, then lifted and scattered, joining the seagulls.

His eyes began to focus again. He swayed. He lurched.

Too late I realized he still had strength left. One of the claws descended, clutching at me, catching my cheek.

I stepped back and he fell at my feet.

I shot him twice more, missing the first time (I was trembling, trembling) but getting him in the back of the neck the second, plumb in the apex of that old-fashioned hair style, which, well greased, had kept its shape even in that wind.

Then I looked around again. Still no signs of life apart from the birds.

I found a piece of driftwood and began to dig into the sand. Too soon, I hit rock. So I contented myself with scraping the sand over him instead. It served. It was wet. It clung.

From the picnic area you couldn't have spotted a thing.

It wasn't until I got back in the car that I noticed the scratches on my cheek. They looked nasty. I thought of his nails. There was no point in taking risks. I went back to the shore and walked out as far as the rippling edges of the waves. I didn't even glance toward the rocks. The balance again. A feeling of utmost sureness. Only this little local difficulty. But salt water is antiseptic, they say. It stings too, I can now say. Anyway, it would have to do until I reached a suitable place on the way back, a men's room somewhere.

Back in the car again, I noticed the bloodstain on my left sleeve. My own? Or his? But what did it matter? I wasn't prepared for another gusty trudge to the water and besides, even if it was his—wouldn't it make a splendid bit of evidence to forward should there be another Schumaker?

As I drove away I looked back at the old Chevvy. Battered enough to have been dumped there. I wondered how long it would be before anyone investigated. How long before the body was discovered.

Long enough, I decided, as I swung out past the deserted ticket booth.

Then another thought struck me. A bonus indeed. For when I

came to think about it I wouldn't have put it past that leering bastard to have made a mental note of my car number. For future reference. A point I *hadn't* covered.

Oh well. It was covered now all right. With wet sand.

I began to sing again, the first time in months.

"A Life on the Ocean Wave."

Her Journal:
Entry Number 21

Has he really done it this time?

Writing all that, copying all that down steadied me up some but now my pencil's shaking again, please excuse scrawl, I can hardly hold it.

Hold it.

Her Journal
Entry Number 21 (continued)

Better.

I never thought I'd be one of these women like Brenda Hunter sneaking drinks in the middle of the afternoon but I needed that, I really truly did. Medicinal. Truly medicinal.

Because it's one thing reading things like that, I mean it's bad enough for any wife to read that sort of thing in her husband's own handwriting in a secret diary, all those details, even if it is all in his mind, but honestly, even though you'd have thought reading it and then copying it would have prepared me in a way, I screamed, I actually screamed out loud when I went down there to put the book away and

Excuse me.

Her Journal:
Entry Number 21 (continued)

Better.

Take a grip on yourself, Pat, there's bound to be an explanation, well there *is*, of course there is, you just said it yourself, the minute you stopped panicking and had another little nip and you began to steady up you could see it in a flash.

Even so. It's no wonder I screamed. The wonder is I didn't scream louder, that would have been *great*, screaming like that and having someone come running in, Sue Grady maybe, she could have heard, and found me down there with, steady girl, with the gun in my hand and my knees all electrical and my ears rushing and booming like there were seashells clapped against them and lights flashing in my eyes.

Yes.

Because there is an explanation, isn't there?

But begin at the beginning, Pat, that's always the best, and yes, it steadied me just copying it all down and when I'd finished I thought the sooner this goes back in the box the better because you never know, he doesn't usually come home early from the office especially after a trip, but someone sick as that you never know and it's always best to be on the safe side.

So down I went and I was just putting the book back in the bottom drawer, label side up and on the left exactly, but *exactly*, as you found it, when I thought about the gun he'd written about, and I was so steady by this time I thought, "Ah, now I have got you, mister, because if you had bought a gun the way you said you had, this is where you would stash it and it's not here so how about *that?*"

And then I thought, "Or is it?" and I began to feel a bit trembly again, because there are two more drawers besides that bottom one.

"Oh pull yourself together, girl," I told myself. "There's only one way to make sure. Why don't you open them and see?"

So I pulled open the top one and there was nothing in there but rows of drills all shining all different sizes but neat as ever all in order and I said: "There!"

And somehow that gave me heart and strength and I didn't even hesitate, I pulled open the middle drawer my woman's intuition telling me there'd be nothing *there* that shouldn't be either.

Well.

My woman's intuition was wrong.

The first thing I saw, folded in a thick bundle, was the girdle.

Well now that pulled me up at first because I'd clean forgotten all about that, but you know what? Bad enough though that seemed when I read about it the first time (is it really only a few days ago?) —bad enough though it seemed then, it came as a relief now, like seeing an old friend walk along when you're in trouble over something, and I even smiled.

But the moment I touched it I knew it wasn't all girdle. Either he'd wrapped it around a hammer or something—but of course who was kidding who, I knew even then while I was thinking hammer that this was something very different.

And it was.

And I screamed.

I don't know much about guns but it looked like the one he'd written about all right, wrapped in the bit of plastic inside the girdle and I thought, "Oh God. It's true. It is all true every word of it!" and I thought I was going to faint.

Then all I wanted was to get it back, out of sight, locked away. I didn't stop to see how many bullets it had fired, or if it had any in it at all, or even if I could find the carton of extras he'd written about. I just wrapped it up again, plastic then girdle, I had enough sense for that, but whether the handle of it was to the left and the barrel pointing to the right or the other way round I didn't bother, I didn't even know.

Well. I'm calmer now. Much calmer.

Because I mean it's obvious, isn't it, he's using these things as props, he's using them to help feed his daydreams. I mean I haven't even bothered to examine that coat of his properly but I bet if I did there would be bloodstains on it where he said. And I bet that white on his shoes really was salt, out of the seawater.

But there will be an explanation. The blood will be his own blood from that accident to his face and the seawater well so what, he'd get that on his shoes at that plant in Portland probably on the docks somewhere, some wharf, some jetty, sure.

So why are you trembling all of a sudden again, girl?

Because.

Because his sickness is getting worse, it must be, needing these props, this gun, especially this gun.

I do wish he would be back early.

Because.

Because well it's funny. He's the cause of it all, right? Right. And yet I love him so much, I must do, this proves it, that I want him here to comfort me and the funny thing is it *will* comfort me yet you'd think it would be the opposite and I ought to be packing and losing no time or at least calling the doctor.

Oh I don't know.

Her Journal:
Entry Number 22

It's just gone midnight and am I glad *that* day is over. You'd think I would be tired out but no. There he is, sleeping like a baby, smile on his face the last time I looked in, anyone would think he was healthy as a lamb I nearly wrote pig but Ron's no pig God bless him.

It was lovely when he came home.

I made such a fool of myself. The minute I saw him, all beaming, more flowers, I could see these beautiful shaggy different-colored chrysanthemum heads sticking up behind his left shoulder, I didn't have to guess what, I burst into tears.

"Hey, what's the matter?"

Immediately, no hesitation, down with flowers and briefcase and his arms around me.

"Oh, it's nothing. It's nothing, Ron. Oh I've missed you."

"Missed me?" He was smiling again, holding me away a bit to see me better. "But it's only been a few hours. How come you didn't feel like this on Saturday after a whole *week*?"

Rich American voice again. Strong hands. I loved him, loved him.

"It's nothing," I said. "I'm sorry for being silly, Ron. It's—just nerves, I guess."

"Nerves?" he said, still holding me tight by the arms and looking so concerned, so gentle, I nearly started crying again. "This isn't like you, Pat. Has something happened?"

He looked around as if he expected to see some kind of trouble right there in the hall.

I shook my head.

"Let me put these in water right away," I said. "Oh Ron, they're lovely. I think maybe it's because they reminded me of when you came to visit me in hospital after my appendix operation, I cried then, didn't I?"

"Yes, but you were sick then. Hey now, come on, Pat, what is all this about nerves? You did say nerves, didn't you?"

"Oh, it's just"—I scrunched at the stems of the flowers ready for the water, thinking, thinking, usually I'm pretty good at excuses, and then it came, what else?—"it's just Palmers Rotten Point, I guess."

The old one.

His smile broke out again, I could see it out of the corner of my eye.

"Oh, *that!*" he said. He put his arms around me from behind and nuzzled over my shoulder with his chin. "You mean it's getting you down again, huh? Well"—he twizzled me around, holding me off again and looking down at my face, but smiling this time—"cheer up, pet! I have news for you."

"Oh?"

"Yes. I'm home again now, there won't be another trip for two weeks—"

"That's not news."

"And—*and*—that next one might be the last for a very long time."

"You don't mean—?"

"I do mean. I mean the old man was delighted, absolutely tickled pink about that Portland contr— *Now* what's the matter? Why the tears again?"

I shook my head, then leaned forward and wiped my cheeks on his lapels.

"Sorry," I said. "Go on. This *is* beginning to sound more cheering."

"Well I should hope *so!* Because you see it wasn't just the initial fifty thousand dollars. That firm has branches all over the continent and it could mean—well it *does* mean—the beginning of a connection worth millions. You listening?"

"Go on," I mumbled, hugging closer to him, wanting nothing ever to come between us again.

"So that next promotion is nearer than we hoped. He hinted as much today. Raybourn's green, bright emerald green. Understand, honey? By Christmas—well, let's say spring, yes spring, that's the time —we could be living in the city just the way we'd planned."

He could talk about nothing else but penthouses all evening, so very happy, and now he's sleeping like a baby.

So why am I crying again, this is getting ridiculous, Pat.

But this time it is happy crying, well happier, because it all fits, I can put it together now and I can see what it's all about.

That switch in his brain.

It isn't even as bad as I thought. If it was just the switch, out of the blue—suddenly to Happy, suddenly to Depressed—there may be no cure, or maybe a cure too dangerous, high risk, like cutting into his brain. But what happens, I can see it now, it isn't like that at all. Something does have to happen first, something in *line*, something to make him very happy or something to make him very sad or angry. But then what happens is he over-reacts. He becomes even happier or angrier than he should be. So then he makes up for it by making up these *extra* reasons. Maybe that's what they mean by "making up" —in one sense—anyway never mind that now. What I'm getting at is this. Isn't that the way it is with Ron? Isn't that the explanation?

It means he's sick. Of course. Nobody's saying he isn't. But not as hopelessly sick as if that switch went on and off for no reason at all. It's just a question of—whatsit—of degree, of—well, you know what I mean. And drugs should be able to handle that easy enough. These days they should.

Yes.

I've checked it over in my mind and checked again and checked again.

Maybe I will have a word with Dr. Martineau tomorrow. He's not bad really when you get to know him. They say he was marvelous with Gene Piscola. And maybe I can change it a bit at first, to see how he takes it. Maybe I can tell him these things are happening to me, in *my* head, well, *similar* things, and see what he says, and then if he says, "Well, Pat, it's simply a matter of"—oh damn what *is* that word?—"of"—I know—"of *over-compensation*, nothing a little rest and a short course of pills can't put right," well then, if he says something like that, well then I'll go right on and tell him it's really Ron I've been talking about.

Yes.

Maybe that will do the trick.

Her Journal:
Entry Number 23

Oh God oh God oh God!

Just when I thought oh God just when I thought I'd got it all covered all taped all settled too.

When I looked back over what I wrote last night I nearly broke down all over again. Oh God why? Why *us?* Please God, why? Just thinking about it, what I wrote last night and how I felt—but what's the use of that? Think, girl. Think about what you are going to do now not what you thought you were going to do then. Get it down, get it down clear, that helps, you've noticed that these last few days, so get it down. Begin at

Oh God!

This morning when I

This morning when he

Usually I'm up to get him his breakfast but with it being so late last night I overslept and he mustn't have wanted to disturb me, oh isn't that just like him, because he couldn't have known then, that's all he did it for, nothing sneaky, he just did it to give me a chance to sleep my sleep out, but when he did get down he must have seen it and

The facts though, Pat. Just what *you* saw, *you* heard, and that, because somewhere there must be an explanation and you have to be very precise, no guessing, guessing could get you into trouble.

So.

Well.

First I knew anything he was standing there, bending over, and he looked so kind, so gentle, this gentle smile, and he said, "Ah, I didn't really want to wake you, but then again I didn't really want you to wake up and find me gone," and then he kissed me and told me to take it easy today and I said yes and smiled back, remembering what I'd decided last night and how things didn't look so black after all.

Oh God.

He had the paper folded up under his arm even as he came to kiss me. He must have seen it already but

Facts.

I must have dozed off, *did* doze off again because it was nearly ten when I looked at the clock, so I hurried up, showered etc. etc. Those facts aren't the important ones, but *this*, this fact, in the kitchen, was, this fact I uncovered, I mean actually uncovered, with a press of my foot, when the trashcan lid flew up and I was just trying to scrape the scrambled eggs I didn't really have an appetite for after all in there, this fact, and even then I nearly overlooked it, this strip of newspaper, not even a full page, just lightly crumpled but still looking new somehow, on top of the garbage in there.

New York Times is the next fact. *This day's* New York Times is the next fact after that. These facts hit me first, well *tapped* then, tapped me, or I suppose you might say *nudged* me.

Anyway. "Why?" I thought. Still not really cottoning on. Just a game in a way, Pat Bracknell, Girl Detective, the way I used to think when I was a child only then it was Pat Watkins. "Now why should he tear this bit out even while he was having his breakfast? Something he didn't—?"

Oh God. It was beginning to dawn all right.

"—*something he didn't want me to see?*"

I'd seen the hole by then but somehow it hadn't really registered. This neat hole, neat oblong clipped out.

And then I realized. It wasn't so much that he didn't want me to see it but that he couldn't wait, he simply couldn't wait to clip it out and take it down there and stick it in that notebook. That's what. And I stared at that hole. I smoothed out that strip of paper and I looked at that hole that was like a window, and the flashing started again, and the roaring in my ears, and I didn't want to know any more, I didn't want to look through that window, I didn't want to pick up the key where I'd hidden it under the living-room carpet, and go down there and unlock that box again, because I knew what

I should find, I should find the view through that window that I didn't want to look at waiting for me and I didn't even want to think about it any more.

All I wanted was a drink, and I had a drink, then another, straight Scotch, not like me at all, and then the roaring quietened and the lights died down, but I still felt numbed. I had to get out. I had to get out there in the sunshine. So I screwed that horrible sheet of paper up and dropped it, no pushed it, shoved it deep into the kitchen goo, out of sight out of mind and out I went, not bothering about my face my hair just slipping a coat on, just heading for the street, people, normal people, anywhere, then her voice.

"Good heavens, you look white, Pat!"

"What?" I hadn't even seen her. "Oh . . . Sylvia . . ."

"Is anything wrong?"

"I—no." I shook my head, smiled, laugh and the world laughs with you, here's a normal person, normal for P.R.P. at any rate, good old Sylvia. "How's Charlie?" I said.

She was still frowning.

"Oh he's fine," she said. Then brightening up a bit she said, "Why don't you come inside, Pat, I was just about to have coffee," which was a lie because it looked to me as if she was just about to step into the garage and get the car out, their "Number Three" as they're always rubbing it in, and I thought, "Why not? Anything but that. Anything but that view," and I said, "Sure, why not?"

"Oh, I do like your new stair carpet, Sylvia," I said, wanting nothing but this, chitter-chatter, girl talk, even if it meant listening to a lot of bragging. "How long have you had it, it must be ages since Ron and I were around here I didn't even know you'd got it," and then she was saying, "Just sit here, Pat, I won't be long, it's nearly ready," which was another lie because when she went into the kitchen the first thing she did was grind some beans up, "Can I help?" I yelled and just at that split second the mixer stopped and my yell nearly made her jump out of her panty-hose and I had to laugh and she looked quite worried again and said, "No, sit down, Pat, go on, I'll be right with you."

Well to tell the truth I suddenly did begin to feel a bit weak again around the knees and I began to wish she'd hurry up with that coffee, maybe I'd given myself bigger slugs of Scotch than I'd intended, and then I wondered if she'd caught my breath, so oops I thought and good as gold I went and sat down on that *genuine* reproduction

Chippendale or is it Chipperfield or anyway on that fancy chair in there and then I saw it.

Charlie Raybourn, I'll say this for him, he has a bit of consideration for his wife in certain things most men don't seem to think about and this must have been one more example, unless of course it had arrived late or he'd simply forgotten it. Yes. The New York Times I'm talking about. Today's. On the coffee table. Folded back to "foods fashions family furnishings"—trust Sylvia—and I thought oh my God shall I? with her chatter coming through—"And then Shiela said"—no, not here, not anywhere—"And Connie looked *very* dubious, you know the way she"—and yet I thought you'll have to face it sometime—"Which just goes to show"—and of course I couldn't resist, I was already turning the pages like mad, and then I found it, I recognized a picture that was on the strip, some Army officer getting out of a plane, and then, a little to the right, then down, the view, and I began to read it and I began to scream. Screaming, screaming even as I was reading it, and Sylvia running in, and then the roaring and the lights and out.

Out like a light myself.

So here I

Her Journal:
Entry Number 23 (continued)

Even thinking about it makes me go dizzy.

Good thing I'm in bed.

But what shall I do? Whatever shall I *do?*

I can't stay here all day. I can't stay in bed till he gets home. At least I ought to be dressed, ready, ready for

Well. Anything, I guess.

I wish I hadn't let Sylvia give me those tranquillizers. But it was either that or give in and let her call the doctor, and *that* I am not ready for yet. If ever.

"No, please, I'll be all right."

"You sure? You still look very—"

"I'll be all right, Sylvia. Just a tired feeling. Just a little sleep. When Ron comes home I'll—"

But my lips were beginning to tremble, so I pulled the covers up over my mouth and closed my eyes and she stayed a moment then tiptoed out, closing the door softly.

And here I am.

With everything to decide and only another what, three, four hours to decide it in.

Because.

Well. You have to face it, Pat.

Well. There doesn't seem to be much doubt now.

Yesterday, the report said, which means Sunday because it said Monday at the top of the report. Late yesterday afternoon meaning late Sunday afternoon, two boys, their dog, the body. Beach south of Portland it said, and then it said his name, Arnold something, forty-seven years old, longshoreman it said, and that was something they didn't find out until Monday, today it said. And everything. Oh God.

Go on. Make sure.

But no.

Everything fitting.

Old Chevrolet. Two bullets. It even said the number, thirty-eight, and "probably"—probably!—a service revolver too. They don't miss much except the main thing: Suspected Gangland Slaying it said, or something like that. Man well known to the Portland police. Small-time criminal who may have stumbled into something big. Talk of drugs. Also talk of naval secrets.

Drugs!

Naval Secrets!

All he stumbled into was Ron.

My Ron.

Oh God.

Oh God what shall I *do?* He's sick, sicker than I ever imagined anyone could be, anyone I knew, anyone near to me, anyone I loved. Love.

And that's the biggest fact of all.

I love him. Oh I've never loved you more deeply, Ron. Oh Ron, what can I do?

One thing. I shall never never never betray him. Not to anyone who can harm him. I know they tell you in the papers whenever they *know* there's a maniac at work, to inform the police of anything suspicious it's your duty. *Someone* must know, they usually say. *Someone* is bound to have noticed something.

Well now I'm one of those. One of those poor agonized *someones* and by God now I know why never, I don't think *ever*, do any of them come forward.

But you can't just leave it there.

You have to do something.

And being sick, how about him, will he look at it the same way if he suspects I know, will he *know* he's safe with me, just so long as

Well? So long as what?

Well just so long as he agrees to take some treatment, some . . .

Well there *must* be something. Damn it he's not *really* a murderer, not at heart, he's the kindest, gentlest person in the

God!

Her Journal:
Entry Number 23 (continued)

He's here. Now. *This* early. Only three. His car. Driveway. Saw him. Looking white himself. Grim.

I've put a chair under the doorknob.

These notes. I want people to know. Sick. Whatever he does. Want everyone to know. Sick. Needs help. Want *him* to know. Love him always. No blame. Always every minute I have loved you, Ron. Just do as they say, pet. Bless you.

Won't scream. Won't telephone. Will reason.

Calling out for me now.

Will reason long as door holds. Got to give me that chance.

Yelling now. Frantic.

Coming up. Handle. Banging.

Now I will reason. Now, oh God, I don't think the

His Journal:
Final Entry

Clearly there are certain conditions under which the balance cannot possibly be maintained, no matter how strongly established. That much is certain and must be duly recorded.

For who would have thought, yesterday morning, only three days after the most brilliantly successful experiment of the whole cycle, that the ensuing sense of completion, fulfillment, could be destroyed so utterly by nightfall?

And yet it is so.

One hesitates to register too personal a note in an account of this kind—personal, that is, in a way that has no direct bearing on the *nature* of the experiments. But since it has had such an effect on the results, an impact so severe that even now it still makes the experiment seem of secondary importance . . .

I am losing the thread.

To be quite candid, one is really in no fit condition to be making such records, and indeed if there had not been such eminently sound sense in Martineau's injunction to try not to think about it too much, to go about one's business or at least to occupy one's mind in the normal way . . .

Well, this *is* my mind's normal occupation, is it not?

I am losing the thread again.

Yet it does have a bearing, so let us proceed to weave it back in.

One hates to sound the note of self-pity, even if the intention to do so could not be further from one's mind, but the irony of it all is so great that perhaps it will help to exorcise . . .

It's no use.

Pat, my wife, to whom really these experiments have been dedicated, no matter what other impressions might have been given, is sick, and that sickness is such that it has canceled out all the elements of success.

That is only to be expected, surely.

Furthermore, the suddenness of the onset of that sickness must be taken into consideration. Had it been more gradual, maybe then the balance would not have been so easily shaken. True, she had given certain indications the day before, but, as Martineau says, that is merely hindsight. One could not be expected to know precisely what they did foreshadow. Not even he—as he was kind enough to add.

The people *are* kind here. When it comes to a real emergency, their real worth begins to show. The Raybourns, for example. How typical of our neighbors here (for it could have been any of them) that Sylvia should concern herself so deeply yesterday, should do everything she could for Pat and then not hesitate to call—no, not me direct —but Charlie, asking him to tell me of her concern, to break it gently but firmly as it were, in such a way that one did not hesitate to drop everything and return home right away. Back in England, now, there would have been a wariness, an instinct not to intrude, understandable, perhaps, but in such circumstances much to be deplored.

Why mention this here?

Why mention anything, if it comes to that?

Everything seems secondary now.

And yet it *does* have a bearing. One's first instinct on finding Pat like that, paralyzed, comatose, contorted, crouched, was to rage—to wish to God one had never seen this place, subjected oneself to these pressures, gone so far out on this brutally prickly, even poisonous limb. And later, in a less distraught mood, there was still the tendency toward deep regret, a wish that the telegram had never arrived that day back in England, or that it had been couched in different terms, negative.

But who is to say that it *has* been the pressures here that have brought this thing on our heads. It is easy to forget other pressures elsewhere, pressures of a different kind, the squeeze, let us say, rather than the push-push-push.

And after all, it did seem wonderful at the time. Still does. Even *now*, for heaven's sake.

One remembers the tingling, as the words of the cable sank in. One remembers calling the boy back, adding another two shillings to the tip. One remembers being grateful that one happened to be home the day it arrived. One remembers going out, waiting at the bus stop to greet Pat on her way back from a hair appointment in town.

A bright, early autumn day. Three buses. Nearly an hour. But not a scrap of the usual impatience. Then:

"What are *you* doing here?"

"Waiting for you, you nit!"

"Yes but—oh . . ."

The telegram. Her face going white. My own trying to look glum. But of course I wouldn't have come to meet her like that had it been bad news, and all at once she realized it.

"Something *good*? Some *good* news for a change?"

"The best."

"The pools? No, of course—"

"How would you like," I was saying, slowly, holding her shoulders, "to live in New York?"

People staring.

Pat jumping up and down.

Then drinks in the local, planning already, planning, planning. And a walk after that, too restless to stay indoors. A walk in the scrubby little woods at the edge of town—a golden-stubbled edge that day—with jays, dozens of jays, flashing and squawking.

"They're blue over there."

No. One can't regret moments like that.

And even here. Especially since the experiments. *We were winning, Pat.* We just about had it licked.

Did I actually say those very words?

And could she hear them?

Martineau says not. Nevertheless:

"She needs quiet, Mr. Bracknell. Above all else she needs quiet. And we must make tests."

Because, balance or no balance, by God I would have dropped everything, anything, just to be at her side, twenty-four hours a day, as long as it takes. Never again must she be allowed to get into that state, too much alone, too much locked up in her thoughts.

Please God (a) let it not be apoplexy.

Please God (b) let the damage not be heavy if it is.

Please God (c) let Martineau be right in hoping it is nothing worse than hysteria. ("Though it is still a serious matter, Mr. Bracknell, you must understand that.")

I suppose I should have gone to work today, in spite of the Old Man's insistence that I do no such thing. But one must be ready, near the phone, close at hand. The minute she regains consciousness I want the first words she hears to be mine, the first touch she feels, mine, the first eyes she sees, mine. Or at least the first loving words, the first loving touch, the first loving eyes.

Besides, if I hadn't stayed home today I might not have noticed the notebook she'd been writing in, under the bed, where it had presumably been kicked in the confusion.

"It could be very instructive, Mr. Bracknell," Martineau said when I phoned. "Especially if she'd been working on it at the time. Have you looked it over? I guess you will have."

I told him I had indeed, but it was not much use.

"It's all in shorthand," I said. "She used to work as . . ."

But this brought back memories that made me suddenly distrust my voice.

"Sure," he murmured. "But it could be very important. Why don't I send my secretary around to collect it? Then if she thinks there might be something useful . . ."

I was thinking fast.

It could of course be nothing more than transcriptions of news broadcasts, made in an effort to brush up her stenographic skills. She occasionally spoke of preparing herself to augment our income if in fact we ever did take the plunge and go to live in New York. But supposing she too had been keeping a diary, wouldn't these damned dashes and points and ticks and curlicues be almost as effective as the tumblers and clasps and pivots and springs of the lock on my toolbox in preserving whatever privacy *she* desired to maintain? No doubt in that case it would consist of a mere catalogue of grumbles about Palmers Point, her boredom here, imagined slights, that sort of thing—but yes, Martineau was right. There might just be something useful, some small clue.

"By all means," I said.

His secretary collected it three or four hours ago. Said she'd take it back to the office right away. Nice kid. Freckled. Hope to God she finds something.

But I digress.

One gets into the habit of noting every detail.

And now, as if to remind one that others have troubles too, I hear what sounds like a near-collision between two cars somewhere in the street below: screech of brakes, doors slamming, purposeful footsteps getting louder, moving toward a confrontation, to be followed no doubt by accusation and counter-accusation, maybe even a whiplash suit—trouble for someone anyway.

And somehow—though it is selfish of one, I admit—it is a comfort to know that one is not alone. That